"Let's Celebrate."

Lorrie welcomed her husband with a smile, sure that each time with Tom was a celebration. "I love you," she said against his neck.

He smiled in reply and met her eager motions with his own headlong passion. He knew just how to excite her, where to nip and suckle and kiss to keep her breath on her lips and her heart in her throat. He knew just when to unite them and push her over the edge.

"Ahh-ah, Tom," she cried. "Tom."

Dan squeezed his eyes shut and dropped his head into the hollow of her neck. If only he could hear her say his name one time.

Just once.

For fourteen years in the throes of passion, while he'd pleasured her with his body, loved her with his heart and soul, given her his seed and children, she'd cried his brother's name.

"Happy anniversary," he said.

Dear Reader,

Holiday greetings from all of us at Silhouette Books to all of you. And along with my best wishes, I wanted to give you a present, so I put together six of the best books ever as your holiday surprise. Emilie Richards starts things off with *Woman Without a Name*. I don't want to give away a single one of the fabulous twists and turns packed into this book, but I *can* say this: You've come to expect incredible emotion, riveting characters and compelling storytelling from this award-winning writer, and this book will not disappoint a single one of your high expectations.

And in keeping with the season, here's the next of our HOLIDAY HONEYMOONS, a miniseries shared with Desire and written by Carole Buck and Merline Lovelace. *A Bride for Saint Nick* is Carole's first Intimate Moments novel, but you'll join me in wishing for many more once you've read this tale of a man who thinks he has no hope of love, only to discover—just in time for Christmas—that a wife and a ready-made family are his for the asking.

As for the rest of the month, what could be better than new books from Sally Tyler Hayes and Anita Meyer, along with the contemporary debuts of historical authors Elizabeth Mayne and Cheryl St.John? So sit back, pick up a book and start to enjoy the holiday season. And don't forget to come back next month for some Happy New Year reading right here at Silhouette Intimate Moments, where the best is always waiting to be unwrapped.

Yours,

Leslie Wainger
Senior Editor and Editorial Coordinator

Please address questions and book requests to:
Silhouette Reader Service
U.S.: 3010 Walden Ave., P.O. Box 1325, Buffalo, NY 14269
Canadian: P.O. Box 609, Fort Erie, Ont. L2A 5X3

A HUSBAND BY ANY OTHER NAME

CHERYL ST.JOHN

Silhouette®
INTIMATE™MOMENTS®
Published by Silhouette Books
America's Publisher of Contemporary Romance

SILHOUETTE BOOKS

ISBN 0-373-07756-4

A HUSBAND BY ANY OTHER NAME

Copyright © 1996 by Cheryl Ludwigs

Printed in U.S.A.

CHERYL ST.JOHN

is the pseudonym for Nebraska author Cheryl Ludwigs. Cheryl's first book, *Rain Shadow*, 1994, received award nominations from *Romantic Times* magazine, *Affaire de Coeur* and the Romance Writers of America's prestigious RITA Award.

She has been program director, vice president and president of her Heartland RWA chapter, and is currently Published Authors' Network Liaison and a conference committee chairman.

Married mother of four, grandmother of five, Cheryl enjoys her family. In her "spare" time she corresponds with dozens of writer friends from Canada to Texas, and treasures their letters. She would love to hear from you.

SASE for newsletter and bookmark:
    Cheryl St.John
    PO Box #12142
    Florence Station
    Omaha NE 68112-0142

Thanks to:
Pam, for the nudge.
Mary-Theresa, for the opportunity.
Romance Authors of the Heartland, for Monday mornings, second Saturdays and Friday nights.
Giving birth to a career is a lot like giving birth to a baby. You really have to do it on your own, but it's nice to have someone there to hold your hand.

Prologue

Fourteen Years Earlier

"Sometimes I want to take the top of your head off and screw your brain in right." Turning from his brother, Daniel Beckett gripped the wrench and tightened the last spoke on his vintage Harley, his pride and joy, as though demonstrating the procedure. "You can't be serious."

"Never more serious in my life, Danny-boy," Tom replied. "Don't make like you're so surprised."

Dan stared up at his identical twin standing with their father's old duffel bag slung over his shoulder, and shock stole any words he might have come up with. He dropped the wrench with a clang and stood, wiping his grimy hands on the jersey he'd appropriated from Tom.

Tom's dark, troubled gaze swept over the shiny black bike without seeing it and returned to Dan. "I can't stay, man."

He turned and faced the road.

Dan struggled with the reality of just how miserable his brother was here. Tom hated the orchards and the rural Nebraska life, always had. "I know last night was bad. Dad rides you—"

"Rides me?" Tom cut in with biting sarcasm. "He has never, for one second, got off my butt for leaving college. He talks to me like I'm some kind of idiot. Like I'm an embarrassment to him, to all of you."

Dan scrambled for words to keep his brother home. The night before, there had been another shouting match. As usual, Dan had tried to smooth things over and only gotten himself involved in the fracas. Now their father was angry with both of them. "He thinks he knows what's best for you, Tom. Dad wants you to take over Beckett Orchards some day."

Tom swung around, dropping the duffel bag. "I don't want the damned orchards!" he snapped through clenched teeth. "If I stay he'll keep bending me. He'll make me work the farm. He'll make me walk and talk and act like he wants me to." The evening sun was setting behind his shoulder. "I can't bend anymore." His tone changed, becoming low-timbered as he confessed, "I'll break."

Dan's chest ached with a growing panic. Maybe if he'd tried harder, fought harder, he could have made a difference.

"Danny, it's me. Not you," Tom said. Tom always knew what he was thinking.

Dan met his knowing gaze, and nodded. He shuddered to think of his father's reaction to this. Whether

Tom wanted to admit it or not, he was Gil Beckett's pride and joy. Or so it had always seemed to Dan. Then his thoughts shifted and something in his heart contracted. "What about Lorraine?" he asked.

Tom and everyone else called her Lorrie, but Dan always thought of her as Lorraine. The name Lorraine held the air of mystery and femininity she deserved.

Tom tilted his dark head and shrugged. "What about her?"

The offhand question sparked the first flame of anger in Dan's gut. There was a time when he'd had his own eye on Lorraine Loring, but after Tom quit college and came home, Gil had done his best to push a relationship between them, and Lorraine was crazy about Tom. But deep in his heart, Dan had harbored an insane hope that if things didn't work out with Tom, she might turn to him. He shook his head to clear the image. "What did you tell her?"

Tom choked back a laugh. "Tell her? Man, I haven't told anybody anything."

"You're going to leave without so much as a good-bye?"

Tom scraped his jaw with a thumb. "I'm sorry about her," he said. "Dad pushed her on me. I like her," he added quickly. "I just don't want to marry her. Dad told me last week it's time to take on responsibilities, get married. Well, I don't want to marry anybody. At least not until I'm damned good and ready."

"Tell Dad that," Dan coaxed. "Tell him you don't want to marry her."

Tom snorted. "Oh, right. And for once you think he's going to listen? He won't believe the farm isn't my thing. Why would he believe Lorrie isn't my thing either? He'd make my life hell."

Dan didn't argue. He knew Tom was right. It would take something drastic—something more than talk to sway the old man. "Shouldn't you at least tell her?" Dan asked.

Tom stubbed his booted toe into the dirt and shook his head. He looked past Dan's shoulder. "She'll get over it."

Anger seethed in Dan's chest. In the distance a car stirred up a cloud of dust on the road. "If you're going, get it the hell over with then."

Angrily, Tom scooped up the bag. Their eyes met and held. On the outside they were mirror images of each other. On the inside they were as different as night and day. Dan wished like hell he could solve this problem. Wished he could say or do something that would make a difference. But he knew his brother's discontent, and he knew, too, that there were no easy answers. He looked away.

"Dan."

Dan waited for his brother to speak.

"Tell Mom I love her. She's the last one I'd want to hurt. It's just that—" he raised his face to the lengthening summer shadows "—I can't take this anymore."

Their mother's stroke had left her bedridden for the past eight months. "Sure. I'll clean up after you, Tom. I've gotten pretty good at it."

Tom didn't reply.

Finally Dan glanced around. "How are you getting there?"

Tom's old car had needed a new fuel pump for a month. Tom hefted the bag over his shoulder. "Someone will come along," he said with his usual careless confidence.

Dan dug in his jeans pocket, came out with the key to his bike and threw it to Tom.

Tom stared at the key in his open palm. "You've barely paid it off."

"Seems like a good deal to me, trading a bike for a farm."

Tom turned and tied the bag on the back of the Harley. He threw one leg over the seat and started the engine. Levering the kickstand up with his heel, he headed toward the open road.

Dan's brother and his bike grew rapidly smaller until both disappeared, leaving a cloud of dust on the gravel road. An unfamiliar emptiness filled him, one he wasn't sure how to deal with, let alone explain.

Tom was gone. His brother. His twin. Half of himself.

As though by rote, he turned, picked up his spoke wrench, dropped it into the toolbox, and closed the lid. His promise to explain things to their mother, their father, and Lorraine closed in with suffocating heaviness. Dear God, what had he done? What had Tom done?

He slumped down on the dented lid of the metal toolbox. From inside the garage, the radio announcer predicted fair weather for the extended forecast. Tom would have a safe trip. Wherever he was headed.

A fresh shard of anger knifed through Dan's chest. Anger at the sudden twist of fate; at being left behind, which was crazy because this was where he wanted to be; at once again taking on the garbage end of the deal and picking up the pieces while Tom went his own way.

An hour later, he still sat on the toolbox, chilled by the cool evening breeze, his butt numb. He was no closer to an answer. How was he going to tell his father

and break the old man's heart? It was no secret that Gil
Beckett favored Thomas, the son born only minutes
before Dan. Tom had the love and approval Dan
craved, and he'd thrown it all away.

Dan carried the metal box to the garage. He might as
well get it over with. Come clean. Let the chips fall
where they may.

Behind him, gravel crunched. He stepped out of the
garage and squinted at the headlights. The engine died
and the lights went out. There was no mistaking the old
Buick. Lorraine Loring got out, closed the door and
walked toward him.

His heart thundered against his ribs. Not now. Not
yet. He hadn't had a chance to talk to his father, hadn't
planned what he'd say, hadn't come to grips with it in
his own mind.

"We need to talk." Her voice trembled with something strangely like fear. Did she know already? How?
Had Tom done the right thing and stopped by on his
way to the great unknown? The scent of jasmine floated
to him on the night air. His heart kicked into high gear.
Tom was gone. Tom was gone. Tom was gone.

And Lorraine was here.

The breeze loosened a silken tendril of nutmeg-
colored hair from her ponytail.

"What's wrong?" he asked, intuitively sensing he
wouldn't like the answer.

"Tom, I . . ."

Oh, hell. Dan glanced down at the faded jersey he
wore. Tom's shirt. As she often did—as everyone did—
she'd mistaken him for his brother. He opened his
mouth to speak, but she stopped him by pressing her
index finger against his lips. The touch struck him like

lightning and rooted him to the spot. He couldn't have spoken if his life had depended on it.

"I'm scared," she said, tears glistening in the moonlight.

Her fear—and the vulnerability in her eyes—did something queer to Dan's insides.

"Tom, I—I'm pregnant."

The evening sounds faded to silence. Her words rang in Dan's head. She stood in front of him trembling, waiting... waiting for what? His shock? Anger? Rejection?

Rejection. Like Tom's refusal to marry this girl, or anyone? Like his flip "she'll get over it"? Like his leaving? Not that Tom had known, but his actions would be a rejection all the same. Lorraine—and her baby—didn't deserve that.

"Damn," he said, cursing his brother.

"It was just that one time," she said on a sob. "I didn't think it would happen...."

She bit her lower lip and Dan's heart wrenched. "But it did," he finished for her.

She nodded. Her gaze touched his and her chin quivered. "Tom?"

He took her delicate shoulders in his hands. It was the first time he'd ever touched her and he liked it. More than he should have, but as much as he'd always known he would. Willingly she came to him—make that to Tom—and nestled against his chest. The tremors in her body arrowed straight to his soul and rekindled his anger. How could Tom have left her like this? How?

Beneath his chin, her soft hair beckoned exploration. He tunneled his callused fingers through the silken strands. Her firm young breasts pressed against him in a delectable fashion. If he was going to tell her, he should tell her now. He could easily grow addicted to her nearness. He'd seen her for years, wanted her from a distance, but she'd been chosen for Tom.

Now this.

The thought that crept into his mind surpassed stupidity. That he entertained it in a rational state bordered on insanity. Sitting on that toolbox must have numbed his brain as well as his backside.

A soft shudder passed through her frame and her damp tears soaked through Tom's shirt. How long he held her, he wasn't sure. Finally sounds entered his consciousness: the motor tinging as it cooled beneath the hood of her father's Buick; locusts in the orchards; a mellow love song from the radio in the garage.

In the end, he really didn't have a choice. No way could he make himself say the words. *Tom's gone and he won't be back. Your baby's father ran off and deserted you. But, hey—you'll get over it.* Had she not been pregnant, had she been someone else, he might have been able to explain things better.

But she wasn't. She was Lorraine. And he wanted her.

She pulled back and gazed up, her expression so lovely and vulnerable it hurt. "I'm sorry," she whispered.

The decision was surprisingly easy. "It's not your fault," he said shortly. "We can get married."

She caught her breath.

"Will you marry me?" he asked.

Lorraine nodded and burst into tears against his brother's jersey.

Chapter 1

Lorrie wakened at dawn and fitted her body along her sleeping husband's sun-browned back. She traced the muscled line of his shoulder with a finger, slid her palm across the warm skin of his side, snagged the sheet with her wrist and continued the caress across his bare hip. She wondered how many times they'd made love in the past fourteen years. Hundreds? Thousands?

"M-m-m," he mumbled sleepily and turned on his back, flinging a wrist over his eyes.

Lorrie speared her fingers through the springy dark curls on his chest and kissed the underside of his biceps. "Happy anniversary."

"Mm-mm," he replied.

She ran her hand across his rib cage and flat stomach. It wasn't fair that his body didn't show the effect of years and children like hers did. While she had a few extra pounds, some silvery telltale lines on her belly, and breasts that could never again be considered perky, he looked better than ever.

She focused her attention on the scattering of silver hairs at his temple. No, it definitely wasn't fair. Thomas Beckett was better looking and sexier than he'd been the day she met him.

He raised his arm and peered at her. Eyes that were such a deep, dark blue that they appeared black from a distance took in her tousled hair and traveled down to the front of her skimpy nightgown, their expression reassuring her that he couldn't care less about the effect of time and children on her body. "What time is it?" he asked.

She glanced at the glowing green digits on the clock on his nightstand. "Five-fifteen. The boys have day camp this week, remember?"

He wrapped his arm around her shoulders and pulled her against his chest. She inhaled the scent of his sleep-warm skin and closed her eyes in pleasure.

"How much longer will the munchkin sleep?" His voice rumbled beneath her ear.

"Probably another hour or so." Their four-year-old daughter, Autumn, woke early with the rest of the family.

"Well then, I guess you have time to give me my anniversary present," he teased and slid the strap of her nightgown off her shoulder.

"How many times do you think we've made love?" she asked, enjoying the touch of his callused fingers against her breast.

"Oh, a couple," he replied, rising to taste the flesh he'd worked to a rigid peak. "Two. Maybe three."

She smiled and held his head to her breast. "We're so good together. Sometimes I think I'll burst with happiness. How would I ever get by without you?"

"You won't ever have to." He slid her nightgown down and away, and his passion-darkened eyes scanned her bare breasts and slid lower. "I'm not going anywhere."

"I know," she whispered and caught her breath when he touched her intimately. "I just wonder sometimes, what my life...oh...would have been like...ah...without you...."

He silenced her with a kiss.

After all these years, he still kissed her as if they were lovers, as if he craved the taste of her and the pleasure he derived from her mouth, her skin, her body.

He rose over her. "Let's celebrate."

She welcomed him with a smile, sure that each time with Tom was a celebration. "I love you," she said against his neck.

He smiled in reply and met her eager motions with his own headlong passion. He knew just how to excite her to the very edge and hold her there in ecstasy for a lifetime. He pulled away completely, giving them both time, and knew just where to nip and suckle and kiss to keep her breath on her lips and her heart in her throat. He knew just when to swiftly unite them again and masterfully push her over the edge.

Lorrie gripped his shoulders, dug her heels into his thighs and rode the crest, reveling in the force of each thrust. "Ahh-ah, Tom," she cried. "Tom."

Dan squeezed his eyes shut and dropped his head into the hollow of her perspiring neck. His heart pounded against her crushed breasts. He kissed her ear, her neck, her collarbone and waited for his heart to resume its normal cadence.

Easing his heavy body to her side, he framed her face with one hand and looked into her honey-warm eyes. "Lorraine," he said softly.

She smiled.

If only he could hear her say his name one time.

Just once.

For fourteen years in the throes of passion while he pleasured her with his body, loved her with his heart and soul, gave her his seed and children, she'd cried out his brother's name.

"Happy anniversary," he said.

Dan pulled out his chair beside Autumn.

"Morning, Daddy."

"Morning, munchkin." He leaned over and kissed her baby-soft cheek.

"Wish I was old enough to go to camp. Can I have Fun-pops 'stead of eggs?" Huge round eyes, the same warm caramel color as her mother's, turned imploring. Her sun-streaked blond hair had been gathered back in a ponytail, and the curling tips trailed down the back of her Barney T-shirt. "Please?"

Dan reached into a cupboard for the box of her favorite cereal. He'd never been able to deny Autumn anything. Lord help him when she grew into a teen. He placed a plastic bowl and a spoon in front of her.

"That was my sock you took," eight-year-old Bram said to his twin brother.

Jori stuffed an orange slice into his mouth unconcernedly. "Didn't have your name on it."

Juice dribbled down his chin.

"Oh, gross!" Bram shouted. "Dad. Jori's bein' a hog again."

"Use some manners, Jori," Dan said dutifully, slipping into his seat. The twins were frenetic bundles of energy, swooping, crashing, charging through life with more zest than the average person could muster in a year. Dark-haired, with honey-colored eyes, they were identical balls of fire.

Dan figured that being a twin himself gave him the edge that no one else—except Lorraine—had to tell them apart. He couldn't tell from a distance usually, and sometimes it took him a minute if they wore each other's clothes deliberately, but there was something about the way Jori held his head . . . and the mannerism Bram had of holding his thumbs and forefingers together. . . . Dan could always figure out who was who, and prided himself on it.

God, he loved them both so much. He couldn't imagine spending more time with one—preferring one over the other. It hurt to imagine it. It hurt to have experienced it.

Steps sounded on the stairs and Thad appeared, tucking in his Bears T-shirt. "Hi."

Thad took his seat across from the twins. With his dark, dark hair, deep blue eyes with thick black lashes, and lean build, everyone commented that he was the spitting image of Dan. And he was.

If you didn't know.

Dan knew. Usually he dismissed the fact, but sometimes . . . like this morning . . . Thad reminded him so sharply of Tom that the sight ripped open a wound that had never completely healed. He wondered if he'd live long enough for time to take such a toll on his memory that the pain went away.

Already, Thad balked at restrictions. Maybe that was just normal teenage rebellion, but Dan was careful not to smother him with responsibilities or talk about him assuming the business. Gil was another matter.

The aluminum door opened and Dan's father appeared on cue. "Somethin' smells good, Lorrie."

"Have a seat, Dad," she said. "Toast and bacon are on the table. I'll have the eggs there in a second."

Gil seated himself at the opposite end of the table from Dan, next to Thad. "All that spring rain didn't hurt the Lodi," he said.

He had an irritating way of stating the obvious. "They look fine," Dan replied.

"All picked?"

"Yup."

"What about the Paula Reds and the Wealthys?"

"The crew got them in yesterday."

Gil leaned aside for Lorraine to place eggs on his plate. "Any fungus?"

"Some."

"Damn!"

"Weather's out of my control, Dad."

"We'll just have a bigger utility crop," Lorraine said.

"Cider doesn't bring as much money," Gil said. "Our baby-food account is our bread and butter."

"They'll get the fall varieties," Dan replied.

"What about the Applejack Festival, Tom?" his father asked. "We usually save the fall crop for that."

"Well, this year we'll just push the cider and jellies," Dan replied.

"And my aunts and sisters always want space to exhibit their quilts," Lorraine suggested, sitting on Dan's other side. "We'll rent it to them."

Grateful for her positive support, Dan met her warm, earnest eyes. She'd gathered her silky hair into a French braid that hung down her back. He gave her an appreciative smile.

Beneath her light tan, she blushed. Picking up her fork, she looked away, and he knew she was remembering their time together that morning.

"Better get used to dealing with the weather," Gil said, leaning toward Thad and shaking his fork. "When the orchards are yours, you'll face this year after year."

"Dad," Dan chided gently. "Thad has plenty of time to decide what he wants to do with his life. He may not want to run the orchards."

"Horsefeathers," Gil grumbled.

"I will, Grampa," Autumn piped up.

Gil scoffed and the twins jostled one another.

Toast popped up in the toaster, and Dan stood to get it, slapping margarine on the slices. The phone rang. He grabbed the receiver from the wall phone. "Hello."

"Hello," a male voice said. "May I ask who I'm speaking to?"

Dan stretched the cord to place the toast on the table. Three hands snatched the slices in a heartbeat. "Who'd you want?"

"I'm not sure," the man replied with a drawl. "I'm looking for someone named Beckett."

Dan dropped more bread into the toaster and depressed the lever. "You've got him."

"Oh."

Dan frowned at the silence that followed. "Hello?"

"I'm sorry. I'm trying to word this correctly. My name is Dr. Vance. I'm on staff at Sisters of Mercy Hospital in Trousdale, Tennessee. I've had a patient in my care for the past couple of weeks. The only link I

have to finding a relative is an army duffel bag with a
serial number. A friend of mine searched out the serial
number. It belongs to a Gilbert Beckett."

Dan's heart stopped. *His father's duffel bag.*

His pulse throbbed deafeningly in his ears and he
turned away from his family at the table. He hadn't seen
the bag since the day Tom left all those years ago.

"Mr. Beckett?"

"Ye—" he cleared his throat "—yes."

"Does the bag sound familiar?"

He glanced over his shoulder and deliberately stepped
into the laundry room away from the family's ears.
"It's my father's. My brother had it with him the last
time I saw him." He bracketed his temples with the
thumb and fingers of one hand. If the patient couldn't
tell the doctor who his family was, did that mean he was
unconscious or that—Dan's mind stumbled over the
thought—that he'd died? "What does your patient look
like?"

"He's a little over six feet. Dark hair. Blue eyes."

Too many thoughts to deal with at once whirled in
Dan's head. "Dr. Vance . . . is he all right?"

"He was in an automobile accident, Mr. Beckett.
Physically, he's coming along quite nicely. He was listed
in fair condition originally and we monitored him round
the clock. He's in good condition now. Ready to be released, actually."

"Did he ask you to call here?" After all these years
was Dan's deception about to be revealed?

"No, Mr. Beckett."

Dan waited expectantly, his heart pounding.

"My patient has amnesia."

The blood pounding in his head must have affected
his hearing. "What?"

"My guess is it's temporary, but we have no way of knowing when or how long it will take for him to regain his memory—or if he ever will. There's no guarantee."

"You mean he can't remember anything? Nothing?" Dan fought back a traitorous sense of relief. This was a terrible thing to have happened to his brother—if it was his brother. What kind of monster would be glad that he couldn't remember?

"Some things. The mind is a strange and complex machine. He knew how to dress and tie his shoes, how to do algebra problems, who the presidents of the United States were, he can sing commercial jingles, things like that. But he doesn't know who he is, where he lives, or what he does for a living. He can't remember friends, family, what kind of car he drives, if he likes baseball or what movies he's seen."

"He doesn't remember us?"

"I'm afraid not."

"Do you think he's my brother? Anyone could have latched on to that duffel bag in all these years."

"That's true," Dr. Vance agreed. "But after hearing your voice, I tend to think he is your brother. I'd like to have you come identify him. Could you do that?"

Dan glanced back at his family finishing their breakfast. It was entirely possible that this wasn't Tom at all. Dan would have to clear this situation up without upsetting the rest of the family. It would be a couple of weeks before the rest of the apples had to be harvested. "I could get away in a day or two."

"That would be appreciated."

"Give me your address." Back in the kitchen, he grabbed a pencil stub and scribbled on the back of an envelope.

"By the way, Mr. Beckett, if this is your brother, what is his name?"

Dan's gaze bored into the back of Lorraine's head. He stepped deliberately back into the laundry room and turned away. "Dan," he replied.

Chapter 2

Dan barely noticed the postcard-perfect scenery of Missouri and lower Illinois. Once in Kentucky, he saw a coyote standing at the edge of the road, watching his red Dodge Ram speed by. When he reached Tennessee, he ran the air-conditioning and as night fell it began to rain.

He stopped for gas and found a chain motel. He'd get up early and have about another hour-and-a-half drive in the morning. After two sleepless nights at home, another loomed before him. His thoughts battled and turned his stomach into a hard lump. Maybe the man he was going to see wasn't Tom at all. He should want it to be Tom, shouldn't he? Shouldn't he be pleased at the thought of finding his brother after all these years?

There was a good chance the patient at Sisters of Mercy Hospital was his brother, however. And that's what scared the hell out of him. He'd always known there was a chance—a very real possibility—that Tom

would turn up. Somehow he'd managed to bury the idea
so deep and so well that he'd never dug it up and examined it.

But now reality slammed around inside his skull like
a steel ball in a pinball machine. Dan lay on a bed in a
room that smelled of stale cigarettes and listened to the
pathetic hum of the overworked window air condi-
tioner. What if this man did turn out to be his brother?

Would he tell him what he'd done? Tom hadn't cared
what happened after he left. All he'd cared about was
getting as far away from Beckett Orchards as Dan's
Harley would carry him.

Dan awoke feeling like he'd been on an all-night
drunk. He showered and dressed and, with his cowboy
hat still slightly damp from the previous night's rain,
grabbed coffee in a foam cup at a drive-through.
Trousdale was a clean little city with friendly people at
the station where he stopped for directions. He located
the hospital and inquired at the information desk.

"Dr. Vance told me to be expecting you," said a ma-
tronly lady with a pronounced drawl. "I'll page him
right away."

Dan seated himself on a blue vinyl bench amidst a
few sleepy men and women and thumbed distractedly
through a sports magazine.

"Mr. Beckett."

Dan glanced up. The man wore a gray suit and light
blue shirt with a tie. He was younger than Dan had
imagined, of medium build with thin blond hair and a
ruddy complexion. He stared through gold-rimmed
glasses with an expression of near awe.

Dan laid the magazine down and stood, removing his
hat. The doctor's pale eyes followed his moves, and fi-

nally he spoke again. "There's obviously no need to have you identify my patient."

Dan's heart thudded. "It's him?"

"I've never seen a more amazing likeness in my life." Dr. Vance offered his hand. "At first I thought there was some mistake and that my patient had come down here to the waiting room."

Dan shook his hand. Well, that cinched it. The patient upstairs was Tom. He wiped his palms nervously on his jean-clad thighs. Now what?

"I'll fill you in on the specifics on the way up." Dr. Vance led the way down a corridor to the elevators.

Twenty minutes later, Dan waited outside Room 316 while Dr. Vance prepared Tom for his visit. A pair of young nurses did a double take when they passed him in the hall.

Dr. Vance appeared again. "This may be the catalyst your brother needs to regain his memory. I'd like to stay to see his reaction."

"Sure." Dan walked past an empty bed and around a curtain. Tom sat in a chair, one stockinged ankle crossed over the opposite knee. Beneath his hospital gown he wore a pair of jeans. His right arm lay against his chest in a blue fabric sling, a cast visible to his knuckles. With his left hand pushing against the arm of the chair, he stood and stared at Dan.

A spontaneous reassurance he hadn't been expecting suffused Dan. Tom was okay. Tom was safe and alive and looking just as Dan had imagined he would.

Fourteen years had planted several gray hairs in Tom's glossy dark head. A few spidery lines radiated from the corners of his eyes, and a fresh pink scar nicked the corner of his chin.

Tom was back.

"I thought you were exaggeratin', Doc," Tom said with the same drawl the nurses used. He stepped around Dan hesitantly, flipped on the bathroom light and gaped at himself in the mirror. Then he stared back at Dan.

"Does Mr. Beckett look familiar to you?" Dr. Vance asked.

"Looks just like the face I shaved this morning. But then that's not familiar to me either."

Dr. Vance glanced from one to the other. "I had hoped . . ." he said, and his voice trailed off. "So you don't remember seeing this man before?"

Tom turned off the bathroom light and stood in the doorway. "No. But, it's pretty obvious that he's my brother."

"I know it's not going to be easy for you to leave with him," the doctor said to Tom.

The import of his words sank in. Dan stared at his twin.

"It must feel like you're trusting your welfare to total strangers," Dr. Vance continued. "I'll contact the university in Nebraska and get a recommendation for a doctor. It's important that you continue counseling."

Tom nodded.

"He says your name is Dan," Dr. Vance told him.

"Dan." Tom tried the name out and shrugged. "Good as any, I guess."

The doctor turned to Dan. "There are some papers you'll need to sign before you leave. Financial responsibility, since we have no record of insurance."

Dan nodded wordlessly. Tom was coming home with him.

Tom handed Dan a folded slip of paper. "Got this notice from an impound lot today. Seems we have a wrecked motorcycle to pick up."

Dan opened the paper and read the date of the accident and the serial number and description of his antique Harley. Tom still had the bike.

"He needs a shirt," Dr. Vance said.

Dan tried to focus on the doctor's words.

"Dan's shirt was ruined in the emergency room."

"Oh." Dan's limbs came to life and he returned. "I'll get one out of my truck."

He escaped down the corridor and out into the humid sunshine. Tom was coming home with him. Home to their father. Home to Lorraine. Now what? What in the hell was he going to do now?

Dan paid the impound lot for storing the mangled bike, loaded it into the bed of the Ram and drove out of the state. Occasionally he glanced over to find Tom staring. Couldn't blame him. Must be a pretty scary feeling to wake up one day not knowing who you were, and then have a look-alike show up to haul you away.

Tom had read the Beckett Orchards logo on the side of the truck as soon as they'd crossed the parking lot. "Is that what you do?"

"Yeah." Dan had tossed Tom's duffel bag and plastic-handled sack of hospital toiletries behind the seat.

"When was I born?"

Dan told him.

Tom nodded, probably tallying his age in his head. Intriguing how he knew math and algebra, but not his own birthday.

"You hungry yet?" Dan asked now as they passed an orange food sign on the highway.

"Yeah. I'm used to three squares in that place. I missed lunch."

Dan took the exit and pulled into a truck stop. They seated themselves at a booth and a young waitress in tight jeans and a Western shirt brought them water and menus. She glanced from one of them to the other. "Double the pleasure, double the fun," she sang around a wad of chewing gum.

Tom grinned back at her.

"Thanks." Dan took the laminated menu and pointedly waited for her to leave. She did so with a shrug.

Tom watched her leave.

Dan studied the menu.

"Do you remember the last time you saw me?" Tom asked.

Dan remembered that evening like it was the night before. Like it was one of the Arnold Schwarzenegger videos the boys watched that he'd seen two dozen times. "Fourteen years ago," Dan replied. "The end of July."

"Have we kept in touch?"

The waitress returned and flirted with Tom while she took their orders. Finally she walked away.

"No," Dan replied.

Tom studied Dan's carefully guarded expression. "Am I the black sheep of the family or something?"

Dan shook his head. "You couldn't stand the place any longer. You told me you were leaving, but you didn't tell anyone else."

"I just left. Like that?"

Dan nodded.

"Did you try to talk me out of it?"

"Sure. But you had a mind of your own." Dan found himself using the past tense, as if he was discussing a person who didn't exist anymore. "You have a mind of your own."

"Didn't I call? Keep in touch?"

"Never heard a thing."

"Did I run off with a girl or something?"

"Why would you think that?" Dan asked. At Tom's shrug, he went on. "You've been somewhere around here."

"How do you know?"

"Your accent. It sounds like all of the people I've talked to the past couple days."

"Yeah," he agreed with a nod. The waitress delivered their food and Tom thanked her with a wink. "Tom," he said and the name he'd been called for so many years shot slivers of dread up Dan's spine. "Who else at Beckett Orchards will recognize me?"

"Our father," Dan replied. "Gil."

"Gil." Tom picked up his burger with his left hand and took a bite. "Our mother?"

"She died the year after you left."

"Oh."

"Strokes." A series of them that had left her without any motor control. Dan took a bite of his sandwich and it tasted like sawdust. She had known. Of course, their mother had been able to tell the difference between them. That same night he'd gone to the bed they'd set up for her in a downstairs room of their old house. Her eyes had been open, and she'd studied him as if she'd sensed something was wrong.

He'd told her good-night and kissed her forehead. She blinked in response. He'd never had to tell her who he was. She always knew. Just like she'd known at that moment which brother tucked her in. He'd realized she would undoubtedly begin to wonder why Tom didn't come to see her. Perhaps Gil would tell her that he, Dan, had left.

The next morning Dan had told her the truth. Tears formed in her eyes and ran down her temples, and he wiped them away. "I didn't tell you to be cruel, Ma," he'd explained. "You would have known anyway, so I saved you figuring it out the hard way." He brushed her hand with his fingertips. "I don't know what you'd say if you could talk, but I'll bet I'd have heard an earful by now."

A frustrated prisoner in her own body, she'd blinked.

Dan had confided in her for the next several months until she'd died. Even when she'd been beyond hearing him, beyond recognition, he'd gone to the hospital and purged himself at her bedside. In all the years since, he'd never spoken the truth to a living soul.

"Anyone else?" Tom asked.

"Lorraine," Dan answered. "My wife. She'll remember you. And of course some of the neighbors. Lorraine's sisters. Probably our cousins in Nebraska City."

Tom finished his burger. "You gonna eat that?"

Dan looked down. "No. Go ahead."

"Thanks."

"Do you want to push on all night or stop to sleep and start out fresh in the morning?"

"Well," Tom replied, "I'm still pretty achy in places from the accident. I'd like to take one of my pain pills and get a night's rest."

"Sure," Dan said. "I wasn't thinking."

"No problem."

"Let's check out the map and find somewhere to stop around supper time. I'll call home then and let them know we're coming."

Tom looked up in surprise. "They don't know?"

Dan shook his head. "I told them I was coming down to the agricultural university. The research lab is doing a study on one of my hybrids. Actually we do all the communication by phone and fax, but I made something up about them needing my input on a project."

"Must have been a pretty convincing story."

"Yeah, well, they have no reason to doubt me," Dan said with a fresh surge of guilt. They trusted him. They'd always trusted him.

Tom sipped his cola.

"I didn't want to disappoint Dad if it wasn't you."

Tom nodded. "Understandable."

Dan adjusted his hat, grabbed the check and paid at the counter.

With a last wave at the waitress, Tom followed him out into the sunshine. "Well." He glanced around. "You have the rest of the drive to tell me about my childhood."

Dan plucked his sunglasses off the dash and slid them on. "That'll make the miles fly by."

He started the engine and pulled onto the highway.

Lorrie handed Thad, Bram and Jori lunches on their way out the door. "'Bye, boys! Have fun at day camp."

"We will, Mom." Bram ran back and kissed her on the cheek before tearing after his brothers toward the bus stop.

Autumn appeared in the kitchen doorway with her crayons and battered coloring books. "I'm gonna make a pitcher for Uncle Dan."

"I'm sure he'll like it," Lorrie told her, hurrying to load the last of the breakfast dishes into the dishwasher. "Here, let Mommy put a clean tablecloth on."

She placed a bowl of fresh violets on the table and took off her apron.

Tom had sounded so strange on the phone last night. She'd known immediately that something was wrong. And then he'd told her that he hadn't really gone to the university about his hybrid project. He'd gone to a hospital and identified Dan, who had lost his memory.

She understood why he hadn't told Gil. The old man was seventy, and there was no reason to upset him until they'd known for sure whether or not the man was Dan.

But surely he could have told her. She wouldn't have said anything to Gil. She felt funny that he'd lied to her, even though he thought he had good reason. He'd never lied to her before. Oh, sometimes just silly things like pranks or where her Christmas present was hidden and what it was. But not a real lie.

But then Tom had always been funny where Dan was concerned. He didn't like to talk about him. Whenever Gil or his cousins or even Lorrie mentioned him, Tom had nothing to add.

Lorrie assumed it was because as twins they'd been so close, and Dan's leaving had hurt Tom more deeply than he let on. The situation had been awkward from the very beginning. The family had been in such turmoil over Dan's disappearance that she and Tom had planned a quiet ceremony, rather than make a fuss while everything was in confusion.

Tom had kept his promise and they'd been married immediately, even though Lorrie knew it was a difficult time for him. For her sake and Thad's, he'd finished his classes at the community college rather than the university. He'd been deeply affected, quieter, more withdrawn than usual. Gil had been thrilled with the change that had come over Tom. He'd never seen him work so hard or so long, as if Dan's leaving had given him a new maturity and a sense of family. He'd proven himself a responsible husband and father.

But Lorrie knew a little portion of his heart had gone with Dan. She wondered what seeing his brother after all these years had been like.

"The truck!" Autumn squealed and tore down from her chair and out the back door.

Lorrie followed. Gil appeared from the corner of the house, wearing a shirt and trousers rather than his usual overalls.

Late morning sun glinted off the truck's windshield. The doors opened and two tall men got out. Both of them wore shirts of Tom's. But Tom, who climbed down from the driver's side, wore his familiar cowboy hat and sunglasses. The other brother's hair was a little longer and he held his right arm in a blue fabric sling against his chest.

Lorrie ran to Tom and Autumn followed. He leaned forward and kissed her, then reached down and scooped up Autumn. "Hey, munchkin. I missed you."

"I missed you, too, Daddy. Is this Uncle Dan? He looks just like you."

"Yes, this is your uncle. Dan, this is Autumn . . . and Lorraine."

She and Dan nodded at one another. She'd forgotten how strange it was to look into the same pair of eyes on a different person.

"And this is Dad," Tom said.

Hesitantly, Gil reached out, tears in his eyes. His hand trembled.

Dan shook his hand. "Dad."

Gil lunged forward and wrapped his arms around his son. His shoulders shook. Tears filled her own eyes, and

Lorrie had to look away. Unconsciously, she slid her arm around her husband and daughter.

Dan felt her hand on his waist and pulled her close. She met his gaze, and tears swam in the honeyed depths of her eyes. She was so beautiful. What if seeing her made Tom remember? Dan'd been a ball of nerves the last stretch of the drive, remembering Dr. Vance's uncertainty, wondering if a significant sight or person would snap Tom out of his amnesia.

What would he do if Tom suddenly remembered?

"Sorry," Gil said and stepped back.

Tom adjusted his sling. He glanced at Dan. "Will I be stayin' here?"

"Yeah." Dan stood Autumn on the ground. "Let me get your things."

"Lorrie," Gil said, turning to her. "Do you think we could celebrate tonight? Have a special dinner? A pie maybe?" He sounded like a kid.

"Sure, Dad," Lorraine answered.

Dan grabbed the hospital bag and green duffel from behind the seat and followed his father and brother.

"We have a lot to catch up on," Gil said to Tom.

"Dad," Dan interrupted. "He doesn't remember what he's been doing since he left."

"That's okay," Gil said quickly. "We'll tell you what all of us have been doing, son."

Tom smiled pleasantly. Dan experienced the strangest feeling. Their father thought Tom was himself. He'd never been the favored one, and now Gil was treating him like the prodigal son. Why should he feel any jealousy? Gil was actually welcoming back the twin he thought was him!

Besides, he was a trifle old for sibling rivalry like the kind Bram and Jori displayed regularly. But then, it wasn't quite that uncomplicated, was it?

"Do you remember what kind of pie you like?" Lorraine asked Tom.

He shook his head. "I seem to eat anything."

"Then I have a preference," Dan stated.

Lorraine turned to him. "And that wouldn't be chocolate meringue, would it?"

"It would."

She dropped behind and tucked her fingers in his back pockets, slowing him down. "And what would you do for a chocolate meringue pie, Tom?"

He stopped. Autumn skipped ahead into the house with her grandfather and uncle. "Oh, I'd lick the bowl, or the beaters. I'd lick anything you'd let me, probably."

She let go, stepped in front, pressed herself against Dan's chest and wrapped her arms around him. "I missed you."

He kissed the top of her head and hugged her fiercely. "I love you, Lorraine. Don't ever forget how much I love you."

Supper was a celebration. Dan grilled steaks, and afterward they made ice cream in the electric freezer and ate it with apple pie. Dan, however, had chocolate meringue. Thad and Dan set up the badminton net and the family played.

"No fair," Bram called. "Uncle Dan can't play on account of his arm. Let's do something he can do."

"No, uh, Jori—" their uncle began.

"Bram."

"Sorry, Bram. I'm pretty tired. They put me to bed early in the hospital."

"Were the nurses babes, Uncle Dan?" Thad asked.

"Oh, yeah," Tom replied. "Especially the night nurse. She was about two hundred and fifty pounds of babe, and she smelled like garlic."

The boys laughed and Dan couldn't help joining them. Tom hadn't lost his sense of humor. If Gil and Lorraine had really been listening and looking, they'd have seen through the charade right off.

"I like Uncle Dan," Autumn said when Dan tucked her in.

He kissed his daughter's forehead. "He's nice, isn't he?"

She nodded. "Is he sad he can't remember you and Grampa?"

"I don't know," Dan replied. "I think it would be pretty scary to not remember the people who love you."

She smoothed her favorite teddy's plush fur. "If we keep loving him, will he remember?"

Dan tucked the bear under the covers with her. "I don't know. We'll just have to wait and see."

"Good night, Daddy."

He blew her a kiss and closed the door.

Thad's door stood open, his study lamp still on. Dan knocked softly on the open door and stepped in. "Have fun at camp today?"

"Hi, Dad." He looked up from a desk cluttered with papers, baseball cards, and video game cartridges. "Yeah. We played ball and swam and stuff. It was cool."

"Good. Don't stay up too late."

"Dad?"

Dan looked back.

"Do you think I could get a job? Joe Kenney's dad needs help for his truck garden."

"Thad, you know how much we need your help with the Festival."

"I know, I just thought—well, I've helped all summer and now the Festival's coming up, too. Sometimes I think I'll puke if I smell another apple."

The last thing Dan wanted to do was pressure Thad into something he hated. "I do depend on your help, but I think we could get by without you this time, Thad."

Thad looked relieved for a moment, and then his expression changed to concern. "What about Grandpa?"

"You let me take care of Grandpa."

Thad grinned. "Thanks, Dad."

"If you should decide to help out, I'll pay you more than I have been."

"Okay."

"I love you, Thad."

Thad nodded awkwardly. "Me, too."

Dan smiled and closed the door on his way out. He stood in the hall and stared at the light beneath the door. Thad was so much like Tom. So much like him that it terrified Dan to think of him running off.

A horrible idea came to him. What if Tom remembered, realized that Thad was his son, and they both took off together somewhere? It would kill Lorraine.

It would kill him.

He made his way to their bedroom and stripped off his shirt and jeans. Lorraine entered the room, carrying two cups of coffee. "It's decaf," she said. "I didn't want it to keep you awake."

"No chance," he denied, sipping it. "I haven't had a decent night's sleep in days...nights...whatever."

She undressed, slipped a long T-shirt over her head and crawled into bed beside him. Dan set his cup down, took the elastic band from her hair and unthreaded the braid. She loved to have her head massaged. She purred and the sound made him hard.

"I hope Dan is comfortable." They'd given him the sofa bed down in the family room.

"It's probably not easy being anywhere when nothing is familiar," he replied.

"Tom." She sat up cross-legged facing him and reached for her cup. "The doctors don't know if he'll remember who he is? Who we are?"

"No."

She drank and sat the cup back. "I felt really funny about you lying to me."

His mind jumped to attention. "What?"

"About where you were going. You could have told me."

"I was upset, Lorraine. I did everything as quickly and as I thought best at the time."

"I know. But I still think you could have talked to me about it."

"I'm sorry."

She reached for the bedside lamp. "That's okay." The room plunged into darkness. "Were you done with your coffee?" she asked.

"Yeah." He settled back against his pillow.

In the darkness, his wife straddled him, her silky thighs on either side of his hips. *His wife.* He'd used another man's identity when he'd spoken his vows, broken every promise of honor he'd ever made. She was his wife only in the way he felt about her... only in her mind and everyone else's. He knew better.

Lorraine ran her hands up his sides, kneaded his shoulders and biceps and leaned over him, her hair draping his chest. She smelled of vanilla and freshly washed cotton.

What would she do once she knew they weren't really man and wife? How would she feel about him then? Dan threaded his fingers through her hair and pulled her face down to his, kissing her roughly.

"Tom, not so hard," she said against his mouth.

Sick of that name, he released her head and yanked her nightshirt up, covering her breasts with his hands. He arched upward.

With a soft rustle, she tossed the nightshirt aside and her hands returned to his skin. "I missed you," she said.

He didn't want to talk. Didn't want to think. He reached between them and guided himself to her. She eased him inside her slowly, then began a tender rhythm Dan wasn't satisfied with. But he allowed her to take her pleasure at a leisurely pace, stroking her breasts and limbs until she stretched out flat on top of him and paused.

Then he turned her beneath him in a swift motion, ground himself against her and unrestrainedly, desperately, possessively, pounded out his fear and frustration. When she gasped against his ear, when her body tensed and she clutched his shoulders, he covered her lips and stopped the name he knew would fall from her tongue.

Dan, Dan, Dan, he screamed silently against her mouth. *I'm Dan!* With a final convulsive shudder, he took a breath, framed her face and kissed her long and meaningfully in almost apologetic tenderness.

He rolled aside, pulling her with him, and blinked away the sting of tears that threatened to unravel his sanity. Dan held her, her head pillowed in the curve of his arm. She entwined her legs with his and remained blissfully silent.

Later... much later, he slept.

from her cup and enjoyed the morning air and the call
of the birds in the orchards.

Her thoughts drifted back over the day before and
Tom's reactions to his brother's homecoming. He
seemed almost... stilted, somehow distanced and terribly uncomfortable with the whole thing. He did have
similar moods from time to time, but she or the children were always able to pull him out of them.

But this... this seemed different somehow. She
couldn't remember him ever having been as rough with
their lovemaking as he'd been last night. Had he ever
been? Maybe at first. Maybe that first time. They'd
both been clumsy and awkward, and it had been over in
such a hurry. Truthfully, she hadn't been all that im-
pressed with the whole sex concept at first. Tom had
convinced her it was the right thing to do, and she'd
been blindly infatuated with him, so she'd gone along.

But the experience had been a disappointment. She'd
had to wonder what everyone found so titillating about
it. All she'd received from the hurried scene had been a
guilt complex and a pregnancy scare. She still remembered how terrified she'd been to tell anyone, her
mother... Tom. She hadn't been sure of his feelings. All
along suspicions had crept into her mind that perhaps
Tom was only seeing her to please their fathers.

She'd gone to him that spring evening, uncertain of
his reaction, uncertain of the future. And he'd accepted the news without fear or blame or uncertainty.
He'd shared the problem and the responsibility.

And that's when their relationship had changed. Tom
had been adamant that they wouldn't be intimate again
until they were married. They'd foregone a big wedding because of his mother's health and Dan's disappearance. In the courthouse in Omaha, he'd made her

his wife. And that night in a hotel in Kansas City he'd shown her what all the hoopla over making love was about.

And each time since it had only been better and better. Marriage had made the difference, she was certain. Once he'd said those vows, Tom had done everything in his power to make her happy.

And he had.

Lorrie couldn't have been happier. Well, okay, maybe one more baby would have made her a teeny-weeny bit happier, but Tom wouldn't allow it. She'd had a rough time with Autumn, and Tom had been terrified. He'd sworn to her he'd never take a chance like that again and undergone outpatient surgery to make it a certainty.

Since the day was so gloriously warm and fresh, Lorrie bypassed the dryer, hung the laundry on the line and waited for another load.

Dan and Gil appeared from the side of the house.

"I thought you'd gone fishing with the others."

"Nah," her brother-in-law replied, pointing to the blue sling. "Can't do much with this arm. I didn't want to be a wet blanket."

"If Tom has enough patience for the twins and a four-year-old, I think he can handle you," she said.

"Yeah, well, it sounded like a father thing," he said, and sat in one of the wicker chairs. "I don't know if I've ever fished before." He glanced up at Gil. "Have I?"

His father nodded. "We used to fish when you and Tom were boys. You always liked it more than Tom, too. He'd get impatient and wander off, throwing rocks and chasing squirrels."

"He sure has patience now," Lorrie said. "Sometimes when I watch him with the children—especially with the twins—I wish I was more like him."

A pained expression crossed Gil's face. "He's good with Bram and Jori," he agreed.

"Gil's been showing me around," Dan said. "Looks like a lot of work."

She nodded. "From June on, we're really busy. Did Gil show you the buildings where we hold the Applejack Festival?"

He shook his head.

"They're just big barns, really," she said. "It takes a lot of work to keep them clean and all the cider presses working. We even have a gift shop and consignment booths. Want to see?"

"Sure." Dan stood with her.

"Walk with us?" she asked her father-in-law.

He declined, and she led Dan down the gravel drive and into the back of the first building. "This is where the apples are sorted," she explained, indicating the room full of conveyer belts with wooden sides. They paused before glass-encased rooms where vats and other machinery gleamed. "The cider's made in here."

Dan's expression showed no sign of recognition. "Clean and organized," he commented.

He followed her to the next barn. "We rent the booths out," she explained, gesturing to the rows of stall-like structures. "People in the community sell and display everything from antiques and crafts to homemade jams and baked goods. We're packed every weekend."

"Do you have help?" he asked.

"Tom hires pickers," she said. "Gil can't pick anymore, but the rest of us work long days until the crops are in. Our families help out with the Festival."

"Judging from your vehicles, the house and property, it must be lucrative," he said.

She glanced at him. He was a complete stranger, yet he looked so much like her husband. It gave her a queer feeling in her stomach. "We're comfortable."

He turned to her. "Was that rude?"

"How are you going to find out what you want to know if you don't ask?" Lorrie had to smile inwardly. The sentiment was one Tom used often when she was about to lose her marbles from Autumn's ceaseless questions.

They finished their tour and strolled back toward the house.

"Did we see each other much?" he asked.

She gave him her attention. "When?"

"All those years ago," he clarified. "Were you and I friends?"

"Sort of," she said. "Tom and I dated when we were all in high school. I used to mistake you for him all the time."

He grinned. "I can see how that happened. What would I say?"

"You'd tell me where he was."

"Did a lot of people mix us up?"

"Oh, yes. Just like they do Bram and Jori."

"But you can tell your boys apart?" At her nod, he asked, "How?"

"I just know. I bathed them and fed them and rocked them and developed this—this 'knowing.' I just know," was all she could say.

"They're great kids."

She smiled. "Thanks."

"Mommy!" Autumn's shriek carried across the yard. She sat atop her father's shoulders, wearing his cowboy hat, her fingers clutched in his thick dark hair. Tom carried two poles, and behind them Thad and the twins carried the rest of the gear. Thad was entrusted with the stringer of fish.

"I catch-ded a fish all by myself!" Autumn cried, bouncing on Tom's shoulders, the hat slipping down over her eyes. "Daddy says we can eat it for lunch. Can we?"

They converged at the back porch. "You know I was just thinking how hungry I am for a mouth-watering—uh—"

"Catfish," Tom supplied, and handed her Autumn's wet shoes and socks.

"Catfish," she finished.

"Uncle Dan, do you like catfish?" Jori asked.

"I imagine so," he replied.

Autumn squirmed and Tom lowered her to the ground. He took his hat from Autumn's head and glanced from Lorrie to his brother. "Did you have a quiet morning?"

"I did," she replied. "Your father showed Dan around the orchards, and I just finished showing him the sale barns."

"Want to wash Autumn up while we clean the fish?" he asked.

"I want to clean the fish, too," Autumn complained.

"No, darlin', you come with Mommy. I need help getting the rest of our lunch ready. You can help Daddy cook the fish after you take a bath."

"Promise, Daddy?" she asked.

He settled his hat on his head and crossed his heart. "I promise."

"Come watch us clean the fish, Uncle Dan," Bram called. "This is really gonna be cool!"

A look passed between Dan and Tom, and Lorrie wondered at the unease she read on her husband's face. "Come on, Dan," he said, almost resignedly.

The crowd of Beckett males headed toward the garage. She turned to Gil, seated in his rocker in the shade of the porch. If he noticed any of the strange vibes she'd been picking up on, he didn't show it. He smiled in a contented manner. "It's good to have them both here," he said.

She mumbled an agreement and took Autumn into the house. It was only to be expected that there would be things to work out. Dan had left for his own reasons, whatever they were, all those years ago, and Gil and Tom undoubtedly had some feelings to deal with over that. Dan's amnesia only complicated the situation.

Maybe he'd remember soon, and everything would get back to normal.

A week later, Dan jockeyed the tractors alongside the tractor barn and fueled them one at a time. He had a couple of days' worth of mowing to do in the orchards; they would be picking the fall crop next week. Just as he finished filling a tank, the hose jerked loose and spurted gasoline across the front of his shirt and jeans. He cursed and yanked the shirt off, wanting to get a good portion of the job done before the sun got too hot.

Work usually kept his mind busy, but mowing the south orchard, he had plenty of time to think. He'd

thought so damned much lately, he could barely eat or
sleep. Being around Tom and living the lie he had per-
petuated riddled him with regret and guilt.

He hated the self-serving way his thoughts kept running. Tom deserved to get better! He needed help and
understanding. What good were his sessions at the university hospital when everyone was telling him he was
somebody he wasn't?

Dan ground his back teeth together in frustration and
checked the swath the mower cut as he pulled it behind
the tractor.

Knowing the ugly mess his masquerade had turned
into, what would he do differently if he could do it over
again? Could he have convinced Lorraine to marry him
if she'd known who he really was?

He played it all over in his head, as he'd done so
many times, and imagined how it could have been done
had he known what he knew now—had he thought of
all the complications that would follow.

He'd never anticipated the repercussions, never
imagined the tangled web he'd woven for himself. First
there'd been the problem of his driver's license. He'd
simply told the examiner he'd lost his last one. The bureau had compared information, he'd paid the fine, and
that had been that. Incredibly easy.

Tom's signature had been a snap. He'd practiced, but
no one ever even looked closely.

He'd even managed the federal income taxes by having Lorraine sign their joint return before he did and
then using his own name and social security number.
He'd done the filing for the orchards on his own too, so
that no one else saw his signature.

The name on his marriage document and on his children's birth certificates was the one that tore him up.

Dan hit the steering wheel with a fist and cut the engine. The sharp smell of freshly cut grass burned his nostrils until tears formed in his eyes.

He could end up with nothing. No one. He'd always buried the worry of what would happen if and when Tom returned. Now he was living it minute by agonizing minute. Tom could regain his memory at any second. Each time Dan approached the house or looked at his brother or met his wife's eyes, he wondered. Do they know? Had he remembered?

What if he remembered this morning while Dan was mowing? What if he went home and found them all waiting? What if they all hated him now? His father. His brother. His children. His—he choked on the word—wife.

Dan had been trying to ignore the gasoline burning through his jeans into his thighs, but the burn had spread to his crotch, and he didn't think he'd be able to ignore that for long. He'd have to go back to the house and shower and change even if he did lose nearly an hour.

He unhitched the mower and drove the tractor to the house. Lorraine's laughter spilled from the kitchen as he bounded up the porch stairs. He pulled open the aluminum door. She turned from the sink, a smile on her lovely face. "Hi, Tom."

The real Thomas sat at the kitchen table, a cup of coffee in his left hand, his right arm, in the sling, resting on the oak tabletop. His gaze slid to Dan's bare chest. "Hi, Tom."

"Hi." Dan turned into the laundry room. It was just as it had always been: he was working his butt off while Tom was having a good time.

"Whew, you smell!" Lorraine appeared in the doorway, one hand resting casually on either side of the casing.

Rapidly, he stripped out of his jeans and briefs, stuffed them in the washer, added soap and twisted the knob. "You might have to wash these a second time."

"Tom," she chided. "Are you going to march through the house like that?"

He glanced down. He couldn't have kept that gasoline-soaked fabric next to his skin a minute longer, but he probably did make for an unusual sight sporting nothing but his cowboy hat and wristwatch.

She was grinning.

He grabbed a towel from a stack on the dryer and wrapped it around himself. "Happy?"

"Blissfully," she replied, tilting her chin upward in a suggestive, yet girlish pose. He *had* made her happy. All these years, he'd made her happy. Dan knew it in his gut.

But he'd done it with deception.

He ran a glance across her glowing skin, her shiny hair, and the loving smile in her warm honey eyes. She'd been his for so long . . . but not nearly long enough. He never wanted to see the love in her eyes change to something else. Couldn't bear for her to see the fraud she'd really married. The cheat. "Lorraine," he said softly.

Lorrie saw something in his expression that made her uneasy. "Tom?"

He pushed past her and headed upstairs to shower and dress. She stared at the empty doorway for a minute, unsettled by his behavior.

Lorrie shook off the feeling, returned to the quart of blueberries she'd been rinsing and tried to regain the pleasantness of their conversation before Tom had come in. "I think I'll make muffins with these. Tom loves them."

Like the coward he knew he was, Dan stayed away from the house most of the week. He found chores to keep him busy, engines to tinker with, and insect traps to check. The family probably didn't miss him. They had Tom to entertain them. The few times Dan did enter the house at meals and bedtime, Tom was firmly ensconced in the family unit, playing video games with the boys, checkers with Gil, or helping Lorraine set the table and finish the meal.

Dan never approached the house without a sick, nervous fist twisting his insides. Would this be it? The final day of familial bliss? Would the hammer fall and crack his ruse wide open?

Would Lorraine ever look at him again? Speak to him again? Love him again?

One afternoon Dan leaned beneath the hood of his truck and replaced the last spark plug.

"There you are!"

He straightened at the sound of Lorraine's voice and just missed hitting his skull on the open hood.

"I have to talk to you."

Pulling a rag from his back pocket, he wiped his hands on it ineffectually. "What?"

"Whatever it is that's so pressing out here is going to have to wait." She wore her red Husker T-shirt and a dusting of flour on her cheek.

"What's wrong?"

She stopped near the front fender and peered at the engine, her loose ponytail swinging over her shoulder.

"We're having a family meeting tonight. After supper. Think you can stick around long enough?"

"What's wrong?" he asked again, dread gripping his vitals.

"You'll find out then," she replied, and turned to leave. "You won't be late?"

"I'll be there."

She nodded and walked from the garage, her rounded backside nicely defined in a pair of washed-out jeans. He watched her go, his mind racing across all the possibilities he'd already considered a thousand times. Rationally, he told himself that if she knew, she wouldn't be so calm.

Would she?

She'd be obviously upset. Angry.

Devastated.

Dan cleared up his mess and scrubbed his hands and nails at the steel sink in the rear of the garage. When he reached the house, Gil avoided noticing he'd arrived. He went about rolling up the garden hose as if Dan wasn't there, but he knew his father had seen him.

"Hi, Jori," he said to his son on the back porch.

Jori didn't look up from the muddy shoes he was scraping. "Hi."

Mouth-watering smells wafted from the kitchen. Tom stood watching Lorraine slice a turkey. Neither of them spoke as Dan passed. Confused, he continued up to their room, showered and dressed, and returned on schedule.

The dining-room table had been set as though it was a holiday. Autumn was the only one at the table who didn't avoid meeting his eyes. "Hi, Daddy!" she piped up. "I make-ded a house for my dolls today."

Dan slid into his chair beside her. "You did?"

"Uh-huh. It's really an apple box, but I putted on some paper and some of Mommy's sewing scraps and it looks like a house now."

He kissed her cheek. "That sounds wonderful. Will you show me later?"

"Wanna see it now?" She grabbed his hand, prepared to drag him off.

"I think we'd better eat Mommy's supper while it's hot. You can show me after that."

Her face fell. "Oh. I can't."

"Why not?"

"'Cause after we eat—"

"Autumn, would you like some mashed potatoes?" Lorraine asked, handing the heavy bowl to Dan. "I know they're your favorite."

Autumn agreed by rubbing her tummy in a dramatic circle and licking her lips. Dan dabbed a spoonful of the whipped potatoes on her plate.

Supper turned out to be a special occasion. Herb stuffing accompanied turkey, potatoes and vegetables. Lorraine had even made the orange-cranberry relish that Dan particularly enjoyed. He hadn't had much of an appetite for the past couple of weeks, and he was soon full.

He studied her covertly as she whisked away the plates and scraped them. Something was up. He hadn't lived with her all these years and not learned the signs. Perplexed, he glanced from one family member to the next, studying their expressions. Tom smiled at him benevolently.

"Why don't you go sit in the family room?" Lorraine asked without looking at him. "I'll finish up and be there in a minute. Then we'll talk."

Dread turning the meal he'd eaten into a hard ball in his belly, Dan stood and pushed his chair back with the backs of his legs.

"I'll sit with you, Daddy," Autumn offered and reached for his hand.

"Autumn, I need you to carry these scraps out to the cats," Lorraine said.

Autumn released his hand and obeyed. Feeling like an outcast, Dan pushed in his chair and descended the carpeted stairs into the family room. He flicked on the television, thinking he'd concentrate on the end of the news.

One by one, his father, brother, Bram, Jori and Autumn filed into the room. Lorraine finally followed. She sat across from Dan and glanced at the television. "Are you watching this?"

Dan aimed the remote and switched the set off. Silence hung in the room. Jori tapped a pencil against the edge of the video storage cabinet in an irritating staccato beat. Dan shot him a meaningful look and he stopped.

Dan glanced from Lorraine to his father and Tom and back, waiting. What was going on, and how long were they going to prolong it? He wanted to shout at them to get it the hell over with!

At last, Lorraine spoke. "I guess it's time."

Dan ground his molars together. "Time for what?" he managed.

"It seems you've been so busy lately, you've forgotten something," she said.

"What?"

Thad and Gil came through the doorway with cakes at the same time everyone stood and shouted, "Happy birthday!"

Dan looked around foolishly. "Did you know?" he asked Tom.

"I have a great short-term memory," Thomas quipped. "It was only two weeks ago you told me when my birthday was."

He'd had so many other things on his mind that he'd never given the date a thought. "At least it wasn't *your* birthday I forgot," he said to Lorraine.

She grinned and leaned forward with her hands on his knees and kissed him. "Now *that* would have required some intensive groveling."

Dan's chest ached from the recent workout his pounding heart had given it. He raised a hand to brush a strand of hair from her cheek and realized his fingers were trembling.

She noticed, too. Their eyes met and held, hers darkening with worry.

"Open mine first, Dad," Bram said and bounced on the sofa beside him. He shoved a clumsily wrapped package under Dan's nose. Dan accepted it and tore the paper off. A plastic box with a dozen compartments held an interesting array of fishing lures.

"Nice, Bram. I can't wait to use these. Thanks."

The other children were impatient to have him see their selections, and there were gifts for Tom, as well.

Dan glanced at the cakes—one chocolate, one lemon chiffon, just like their mother had baked all the years they were growing up. Lorraine sliced them and handed Dan a huge piece of lemon chiffon.

Dan caught the fork before it slid into his lap and thanked her. Tom took a bite of the chocolate slice Lorraine handed him—*his* cake, Dan thought testily. Tom glanced from one slice to the other and gave him a curious look. Dan's heart missed a beat.

"Something wrong?" Dan asked.

"No." He looked at the two cakes side by side on the oak coffee table. "For a second I thought I got a picture of doing this before. Maybe it was just one of those déjà vu things."

There it was, just as he'd feared: Tom's memory being jogged by the sight of their birthday cakes. What else would remind him? How long would it take for his life to come back into focus?

"Your Ma always made you boys your favorite cakes," Gil hastened to say. "Clear up till..." Dan thought he was going to say "until you left," but he finished, "till her strokes."

Dan choked down the damned lemon chiffon, the same nasty cake he'd eaten every birthday since he'd taken Tom's identity. He wanted chocolate!

Tom shrugged as if he still wasn't sure of the fleeting image and everyone finished their cake and ice cream and wandered off to their rooms.

Leaving Tom to his sofa bed in the family room, Dan helped Lorraine rinse the plates. Shrugging off his bleak mood before he gave her cause to wonder, he followed her upstairs, where she slipped into the bathroom and returned in a short nightie. "Didn't you wonder why I didn't give you anything?" she asked.

He had. "You don't have to give me anything."

She got into bed. "Okay."

He used the bathroom and came back to find her reading. Such a deceptively ordinary scene. He plucked the paperback from her hands and held it behind his back. "Good book?"

She snuggled into the covers. "M-m-m-h-m-m, but I was getting sleepy."

He dropped the book on her nightstand and climbed over her, making certain he jostled her on the way, and slid under the covers, then he reached up and turned off the light. "'Night."

She flung up and switched on her lamp. "Oh, all right!"

"What?" He rolled back and gave her his most innocent look.

She reached under the bed and pulled out a small package.

Dan sat up, reaching for it. "For me? Why, you shouldn't have!"

"All right." She tried to snatch it back, but he held on and pushed her back with one arm.

The square gift was surprisingly heavy. He tugged the ribbon free, peeled off the paper and opened the box. Inside was a brass apple paperweight. Engraved on the crest were two linked hearts and the words, "Two Hearts That Beat As One."

Dan looked up. Her cheeks were pink. The words were from a song they'd danced to as newlyweds. "Corny, huh?" she asked.

Shame, like a rusty blade, carved a ragged crater where he'd once had a heart. She had entrusted him with her heart, her love, her children, her livelihood. She'd given herself unsparingly and without reservation or question. She was the most beautiful woman alive, the most precious creature who'd ever breathed.

And he had defiled her love and trust with lies.

She deserved more. She deserved better. She deserved ... the truth.

The truth.

Dan's throat grew tight with the paralyzing thought. A numbing fog wrapped around his brain and filtered out all but the terrifying concept. He had to tell her.

He couldn't go on like this. He couldn't live each day, each hour, each minute waiting for the other shoe to drop. Eventually, if Tom didn't remember first, Dan would lose his mind. The idea whirled around in his head and left him pathetically devoid of anything but the tormenting thought of losing Lorraine—and her love.

"You don't like it." She lowered her eyes.

He placed a knuckle under her chin and raised it until her eyes met his. "I love it."

"Really?"

"Really." He couldn't tell her right now. He would tell her tomorrow. He'd find somewhere for the children to go for the day and he'd tell her then. While they were alone. With plenty of time to talk and...and what...?

All he knew for sure was that he couldn't survive any more days and nights like these.

She wrapped her arms around his neck and kissed him. Leaning to place the gift and wrappings on the floor, he pulled her into his arms and lay back. She turned and plunged the room into darkness again. This time the teasing was over. She ran her palms across his chest and down his belly. He caught her hands in one of his and brought them to his lips.

"Tom?" she asked.

He let go of her hands and covered her lips with his fingers. "Sh-h-h."

He knew his lack of response puzzled her. He was always ready for her touch, eager for their lovemaking. But tonight he just wanted to hold her. "I love you,

Lorraine," he whispered. "Don't ever forget how much I love you."

She snuggled her head under his chin. Moonlight seeped through the half-closed mini-blinds and cast silver bars across her slender bare legs and feet. Her wonderful fresh jasmine scent stabbed him with sorrow. With reverent fingers, he stroked her thick, silken hair and knew when she fell asleep. *Sleep, my love. You need your rest.*

He needed to have her close now. Now while she still needed him, still loved him, still thought her life was secure and happy. *Sleep, my sweet Lorraine. Tomorrow I'm going to tell you something that will hurt you more than anything you've ever known. Tomorrow I'm going to break your heart.*

Chapter 4

"I can't believe how much they eat!" Lorrie said as the boys slammed out the back door after grabbing a box of granola bars almost as soon as breakfast was over.

"We'll need drinks for the pickers on Monday," Tom said. The crew brought their own lunches, but Lorrie provided coolers of tea and lemonade all day long.

It was unusual to see her husband sitting at the kitchen table with a newspaper and a cup of coffee. Autumn skipped into the kitchen and he lifted her into his lap. "Why don't you go on into town for groceries," he offered. "Autumn and I will play until you get back."

Autumn grinned and clapped her hands.

"Don't you have work to do?" Some mornings recently, he hadn't even stayed around long enough for breakfast.

"I'd like some time with her."

Lorrie didn't need a second invitation to do her shopping alone. When she returned, the children were nowhere in sight, and Tom helped her put the groceries away. "Where are the kids?"

"I took them to your mom's for the rest of the day."

She straightened from placing fruit in the drawer in the refrigerator and turned to look at him. "You what?"

"I called your mom and drove them over. She didn't mind. In fact, she asked if they could spend the night and go visit your Aunt Bernice with her tomorrow."

"And?"

"And they packed a change of clothes and their toothbrushes and they're gone."

She tucked a strand of hair behind her ear. "Criminy, what will I do with myself all day?"

He folded a paper sack and slid it between the counter and the fridge without meeting her eyes. "I had a purpose."

She shut the refrigerator door and studied him. "What's that?"

"I wanted some time alone with you."

She dropped her gaze to the navy Cowboys T-shirt molding his solid chest. "Why, you devil."

Tom plucked a jar of peanut butter off the table and sat it inside the cupboard. "Dad and Dan went to a horse show at Aksarben. He said they'd eat supper in the city and visit my aunt this evening."

They would be in Omaha all day. She and Thomas really were alone. "What did you have in mind?"

He folded another sack.

"Want to run naked through the house or something?"

He didn't smile at her suggestion as he should have. The sack fell still in his hands and a little ripple of concern eddied through her chest. He held his jaw so taut his teeth must have ached. "We have to talk."

A feeling of foreboding settled over her. Intuitively, she knew it had something to do with his restlessness since Dan's return. "This is serious, isn't it?"

"Yeah." He laid the bag back down. "It's serious."

Fear took possession of Lorrie's senses. Apprehension coiled in her stomach. Something was wrong. Terribly wrong. She'd never seen her husband like this. "Well?" she asked, not willing to wait another moment.

"Come on." He grabbed his hat from the hook inside the laundry room. "Let's go outside." She followed him out the door and across the porch.

She walked beside him across the yard and up a slope to a stand of peach trees. Lorrie gazed up into the branches and waited for him to speak. Her stomach knotted. He'd been acting so odd . . . what could possibly be— A sick, gripping dread seized her and she shot him a glance. "You're not—" Lord, she couldn't even find words for it! "There isn't someone else?"

Tom's mouth fell open. "No! Of course not! Why would I look twice at anyone else? For God's sake, Lorraine, when would I have the time or the energy?"

She shrugged one shoulder foolishly, but in relief. "I don't know. It was the worst thing I could think of."

"Sit down," he said.

Without argument, she sat on the ground in the shade. Well, if it wasn't another woman or a mid-life crisis, it was something they could handle together. They'd always handled everything together. "Is it the orchards, Tom? Are we in trouble?"

He did all the bookkeeping on his own, always had, even though she'd offered to share the task.

"No." He paced in front of her for a full minute.

She waited.

He stopped.

She looked up.

"I'm not Thomas." He observed her from beneath his hat brim.

She waited.

"I'm Daniel."

She waited for him to make sense.

"I'm not Tom. I'm Dan," he repeated.

She didn't even have to look twice. "Dan has a scar on his chin and a broken arm," she replied.

"No. *Tom* has a scar on his chin and a broken arm."

What was the joke? Whatever it was, she didn't get it. "Tom, I—"

"I'm not Tom," he interrupted. He squatted down in front of her. "I'm Dan."

Puzzled by this outrageous game, she didn't know how to respond. "I don't know what this is supposed to prove, but I know who you are. You couldn't trade places with your brother and fool me for a minute. I'm your wife, remember? You'll have to pull this one on somebody else." She started to rise.

"No." He pushed her back down with his hands on her shoulders. "You have to listen. I have to say this. I can't live like this anymore."

His voice had a desperate tone she didn't recognize, a tone that numbed her with fear. She sat back and studied him warily.

"I am Dan. Fourteen years ago when Tom told me he was leaving, I handed him the keys to my bike and watched him go. He left without a backward glance at this place or a word to you or my parents."

He took his hands from her shoulders and hung his elbows over his knees, forearms dangling. "That same night you came and told me you were pregnant. I let you think I was Tom. I pretended to be Tom. I've pretended to be Tom all these years. But I'm not. I'm Dan."

Still she stared at him, trying to understand why he would say something so outrageous. "I don't know why you're doing this," she said. "But it's absurd. You can't really expect to get a reaction from me."

"Lorraine, I'm telling you the truth. The man you were going to marry left that day. I took his place."

"I don't believe you."

He stood. He ran his hand over his face in frustration, then raised his palm to her. "Wait here."

He ran toward the tractor garage.

Afraid, Lorrie watched him disappear. What was wrong with him? Should she take him to a doctor?

He loped back up the hill and dropped to his knees in front of her. A curved wallet with worn edges lay in his hand. He opened it and slid out a driver's license.

She took it from him. It was Dan's. A photo of a much younger Dan stared back at her. "See," he said. "Here's my social security card, a sports I.D. pass, a library card. Look."

She did. She examined each item he handed her. "How did you come by Dan's wallet?" she asked, knowing it hadn't been used or updated in all these years. "What did he do without it?"

"It's mine," he explained again, patiently. "I hid it and told everyone I'd lost it. I got a new driver's license in Tom's name."

Lorrie studied the license in her hand and finally looked up. He really believed this. He was sincere. For a moment, his earnest story and the fear in his eyes almost made her believe it, too. "All right," she said. "Let's say, for the sake of argument, that this was true."

His mouth thinned into a line.

"And if you were Dan, why would you have done it?"

Dropping the wallet on the ground, his hands fell to his knees. He studied something over her shoulder distractedly. "Tom had everything," he said softly. "Dad was crazy about him, even though he didn't want any part of the orchards or small-town life. You were crazy about him."

How could he speak this convincingly about himself as though he were someone else? Confusion overshadowed logic in Lorrie's head.

"He had Dad's attention, he had you, he had the orchards... but he didn't want any of it. Don't you remember how Tom avoided this place? How the trees and the work bored him? How he talked of getting away? If the real Tom had stayed, would he have suddenly grown a love for the orchards? Would he love this place like I do?"

"Why wouldn't we have noticed a change like that?" she asked, more afraid than ever.

"Because you wanted to believe it. Because my father wanted to believe it. If the real Tom had stayed, would he have loved you like I do?" he added.

"You're frightening me," she whispered.

He touched her face and his hand shook.

"How could we not have known?" she asked, as
though still merely considering whether this could have
happened.

"Once he was gone, it was easy to be more like him,"
he said. "People see what they want to see. Except my
mother. She knew."

"She knew?" Lorrie echoed. Like she herself in-
stinctively knew her own boys apart?

He nodded, and to her distress tears came to his tortured blue eyes. "She couldn't talk, and it was so unfair of me to make her suffer like that, but it was done.
In the space of a heartbeat, I made a decision that will
hurt all of us until the day we die."

His voice trembled and her heart quaked.

"But, Lorraine?" he said and met her stare. To her
pure horror, pain and regret were reflected a thousand-
fold in his eyes. "I can't really be sorry. I treasure every
moment I've spent with you in all this time. You're my
life."

It hit her then, like a wrecking ball toppling a building. He was dead serious.

And he wasn't insane.

Her heart stopped.

"You're telling the truth," she said.

"Yes."

"I didn't marry Thomas Beckett."

"No."

"You're Daniel."

"Yes." He released a breath almost like a sigh of relief.

For several minutes she didn't really feel anything.
She could smell the earth, feel the grass beneath her,
hear the birds in the branches nearby. But she'd lost all
emotion.

Tom sat back on the ground in slow motion. Not Tom. *Dan.* "What about—him?" she asked. "Your brother."

"He's the only person on earth besides myself who really knows," he said. "And he can't remember."

"But when he remembers, he'll know he's—Tom."

He nodded.

Slowly the numbness dissipated. An ache she knew could never be soothed gaped in her chest. Horror filled her vision and denial sprang to her lips. She leapt to her feet. "You're lying!" she screamed. "You're lying!"

"No, Lorraine." He rose to his knees again. "I'm—"

"I don't know why you're doing this! You're crazy! Or you're sick! This is some crazy, sick joke, and I'm not going to listen to any more of it!" She spun on her heel and ran blindly toward the house.

"Lorraine!" he called.

She ignored him and ran on.

"Lorraine!"

She stumbled and sprawled in the grass.

"Lorraine, honey," he crooned, kneeling over and reaching for her. His hat tumbled over her head. "Baby, I—"

"No!" She rolled aside and scrambled to get away from him. "You're lying!"

They both stood. "You know it's the truth," he rasped. "You know it."

Anger exploded inside her. She balled her hands into fists at her sides. "You're a liar!" she screamed.

He faced her. "Yes."

"You lied to me," she said, her voice quaking with fury. "You lied to me every minute of every hour of every day! You made our whole life a lie!"

"Yes," he said.

Everything had been a lie. Her marriage was nothing but a mockery. All this time he had deceived her. All these years she'd thought she was married to a man only to learn it wasn't really him. Why? What had he hoped to gain from the travesty? "You're a selfish, lying bastard," she hissed.

"Yes," he replied.

She reached out and slapped him hard.

As if it were his penance, he stood there, with his face turned to the side, a red welt forming across his cheek.

She slammed both fists into his chest and he staggered. She hit him again. And again. He held his mouth in a firm line, but didn't flinch.

Lorrie thrust her fingers into her hair and clutched her scalp painfully. "Oh, God," she wailed, dropping to her knees.

He reached for her.

"Stop it!" She slapped his hands away. "Don't touch me!" Anger dissolved into wretched grief. On her knees, she curled her fingers into the grass and sobbed, her hair falling loose and hanging to the ground. "Oh, God," she cried helplessly. She sobbed until her throat ached and her eyelids felt like sandpaper.

Finally, what seemed like hours later, she sat back on her haunches, raking her hair back with one hand. He sat a few feet from her, legs bent, his head buried in the arms he'd crossed over his knees. At her silence, he raised his head. He looked like she felt, lines etched beside his mouth, his eyes red.

She'd thought she knew every line and plane and curve of his beloved face. She'd loved every familiar expression. But she'd been in love with an illusion. She didn't even know who he was. He was a stranger.

"What are we going to do?" she asked around the despair in her throat.

He rested his head on his hand. "I don't know."

"What did you think would happen?" she asked incredulously. "What ever crossed your mind to consider such a cruel thing?"

"I didn't do it to be cruel, Lorraine."

"Then why? Why did you do it?"

"I thought it would break your heart when you found out he left. I thought it would break my father's heart. I had made up my mind to tell you, but then . . . you came to me that night . . . and you were so frightened. I couldn't do it."

"So you spared me a broken heart?"

He didn't seem to have an answer.

"What do you think *this* feels like?" she asked in a hoarse whisper.

They sat in silence for endless minutes.

"You felt *sorry* for me?" she asked finally, never having felt so ashamed, so humiliated and embarrassed.

"No, Lorraine," he said, raising shimmering eyes. "I loved you."

A long silence followed, while both of them thought and hurt and wondered if their lives would ever make sense again.

"So," she said, thinking aloud. "You pretended you were—Tom, and we got married."

He remained silent.

"And on our wedding night . . ."

He looked up.

"That was the first time we . . . ?"

He nodded.

She actually felt embarrassment warm her skin. "And I didn't know the difference."

"I thought you would," he said. "I was terrified that you'd know then."

She shook her head, more of it making sense to her now. How could she not have realized? He'd been more reverent...more respectful...and she should have known something that important—that personal. "He and I only...it was just that once...in the dark and it was over quickly."

"I couldn't believe you didn't know," he said.

"I didn't. I didn't have much to compare it to."

"I was so afraid of—of giving myself away somehow. But amazingly, it didn't happen. I figured if I could get through that, I could get through anything," he admitted. "The times you mentioned—being with Tom, I died inside. I pretended to know what you were talking about, but I hated the thought of you and him."

"I thought getting married must have made all the difference," she said, feeling like a fool.

He straightened his shoulders as if he expected her to hit him again. As though he deserved it. As though it would make her feel any better.

She brought a hand to her mouth and caught a sob she hadn't known was left inside her. "Oh, God."

She collapsed on her back and stared sightlessly at the blue sky overhead. She'd built her whole world around this man. This intimate stranger.

A fluffy white cloud passed overhead. The breeze ruffled her hair.

"I had to tell you," he said. "I couldn't live another day wondering...waiting...knowing that he could remember at any minute...and then you would hate me."

The grass rustled as he moved closer. "Lorraine, do you hate me?"

He remained close without touching. "I don't know," she answered, truthfully. "I really don't know anything right now, and I never did. I can't tell what I think or how I feel." She sat up. "No, that's not true," she said, hearing her voice grow stronger. "I'm madder than hell. The only thing I'm sure of about you is that you're a liar and you can't be trusted."

She stood, not caring how hurting her words were. "I'll never forgive you."

She didn't want to look at him—couldn't. Leaving him sitting in the grass, she ran back to the house.

He entered the silent house at mealtime, not really expecting anything as normal as supper. He found her slumped on the window seat in their bedroom, still wearing the same grass-stained jeans, her hair still uncharacteristically tangled across her shoulders. "Are you all right, Lorraine?" he asked.

She stared out the open window without turning toward him. When she spoke, her voice was hoarse. "He used to call me Lorrie. Dan—you...you're the only one who ever called me Lorraine all the time."

Because he'd always thought of her as Lorraine. Mysterious. Feminine.

He perched on a brocade chair and glanced around at the pieces of their history, the furnishings they'd chosen together. The lamp from an auction. He thought it looked like something from a Star Trek set, but she loved it. The armoire they'd inherited from her aunt and turned into an entertainment center. The white stone fireplace sat as cold and empty as his heart now, but he couldn't count the times they'd cuddled before its warmth, made love with the heat of its fire caressing their bare skin.

They'd planned this room together, going over all the special details with the contractor. After sharing a small, drafty room with a crib in the old house, this had been their haven.

"How are we going to handle this?" he asked.

She turned to him, her lovely eyes dull, the lids puffy. "You expect me to help you figure out how to fix this mess?"

He shook his head. "No."

"One of us has to move out of this room," she stated.

No words had ever hurt him more. Nothing could have. "We can't do that," he objected with a desperate edge. His heart pounded. This couldn't happen. He needed time to show her he loved her, make her understand. "What would the kids think? It would only frighten them."

She turned her gaze back to the meadow beyond the house. After a long minute she sighed. "You're right."

Relieved, he stood.

"Why couldn't it have been another woman?" she asked.

Dan thought he'd hurt as much as was humanly possible, but the flat tone of the question defined her hopelessness and told him he'd committed the worst possible sin.

"I could have forgiven you for a woman," she said.

It had hurt when Tom had left, but he'd gone on. He'd been wrong all those years ago when he'd thought Tom was his other half. Lorraine. Lorraine was the air that he breathed, the life-giving water his thirsty soul drank. Her words tore something vital from inside him. The distance she'd placed between them filled him with desperation. He'd never known what hurt was until this moment.

He moved to leave the room.

No. He had to remind himself it wasn't her reaction that was the problem. It was what he had done. He'd brought it all on himself. He deserved whatever happened.

"Lorraine," he said, turning back from the doorway. She hadn't moved, didn't look up. *I love you. I'm sorry.* He had nothing to say to her, nothing to take away the vile thing he'd done and give her back her happy life. They were living his worst nightmare.

He left silently.

Lorraine turned listlessly to the empty doorway. Getting up, she closed the door and lay on the bed—their bed. They'd picked it out together after the new house was ready to move into. It was a king-size, and Tom—she caught herself—*he* always kidded that they might as well have bought a twin for as little space as they used for sleeping. When they *weren't* sleeping, she'd countered, that's when they'd gotten their money's worth.

Tears from a seemingly endless well rose again and she curled into a despondent ball and pressed her fists to her eyes. The fleeting thought that this was an awful nightmare and she'd wake up came and went.

No, she was awake. Outside, the sun was low in the sky. The quilted comforter beneath her was soft, that pillow beside hers—*his* pillow—lay where she'd placed it that morning.

All these years. All these wonderful, horrible years of deception. All the times she'd made love with him, slept beside him, washed his clothes, cooked his meals, borne his children.

His children.

Lorrie opened her eyes and stared sightlessly at the room. Their children. He loved them as much as she did. He was a wonderful father. Hell, he was a wonderful husband! He'd been so frightened when she'd had so much difficulty giving birth to Autumn. The love in his eyes had gotten her through it. And afterward he'd tended to her like a queen. He'd taken more than his share of 2:00 a.m. feedings. Autumn couldn't have had a more adoring father.

While Lorrie recuperated, he'd seen to it the boys were fed and bathed and paid attention to. He was wonderful with the twins. Having been a twin himself must have given him more insight and understanding into Bram and Jori's individual needs, because he always had time and encouragement for them both.

And Thad. Well, of course, Thad had been their firstborn, so he'd been special from the beginning. Lorrie would never forget how proud...*Dan*—the name would never feel right—had been to take the children places and introduce them and show them off.

From the beginning, that very first pregnancy, he'd shared in the wonder and the excitement. He had been there for her in the hospital, coaching her, holding her hand, telling her when to breathe. When Thad had come into the world, all slippery and funny-looking, with a head too big for his scrawny newborn body, Dan had cried. He still looked at Thad with wonder and amazement in his eyes, as Lorrie herself often did, marveling at the fact that they'd created such a fine son together.

Lorrie's thoughts drifted back sleepily, remembering snippets of their cheerless conversation that afternoon. Dan had deceived her because he couldn't bear to tell her the truth that long-ago night, and because he loved her. What kind of love was that?

The thought of her having been with the real Tom that one time had tortured him.

Lorrie's eyes flew open.

Good God! He thought Thad was Tom's son, because he thought she'd been pregnant when they were married! This new horror compounded the ache in her head and she pressed her palms to her forehead.

Her own tiny deception had never mattered. *Never* mattered . . .

Until now.

She hadn't lied to him that night. She'd really believed she was pregnant with Tom's child. She knew now that stress and fear and the pressure her father placed on her had delayed her period.

Once she'd discovered her mistake, she'd been afraid to tell him. What if he'd thought she'd tried to trick him into a proposal?

Shame coursed through Lorrie in a wave. She hadn't told him. They'd married immediately, been so physically attracted that they hadn't kept their hands off each other, and she'd quickly gotten pregnant.

To her husband's knowledge, Thad had only been three weeks late, which was not all that uncommon for a first baby.

All these years. All this time, every day, every time he saw him, Dan had believed Thad was Tom's child.

She pressed a hand to her mouth and wondered for the first time how Dan must have felt all those years pretending to be Tom. How much guilt and shame had tortured him? How many times had he wondered if she suspected, and what would happen when she found out the truth?

How had it been possible for them to live together all that time with a secret of this magnitude between them? If the real Tom hadn't shown up, would he have ever told her?

Hers was an honest mistake. She'd really believed she was pregnant. Dan hadn't really believed he was Tom! Her deceit didn't carry nearly the repercussions that his did. A shudder passed through Lorrie's body.

How could she not have known?

On their wedding night, he had checked them into the Allis Plaza Hotel in Kansas City and they'd had a lovely dinner in the plush restaurant with a waterfall and a pianist in the background. Later, they'd had drinks in the lounge, danced for an hour or so, and taken the elevator up to their room.

Lorrie had gone into the bathroom and dressed in the simple ivory silk peignoir set her sister had given her, belting the sash at her waist. When she returned, the television set was playing softly. The maid had turned back both of the beds, and he sat, both pillows propping his head. He'd removed his tie and shoes, but still wore the light blue dress shirt and dark slacks.

His deep blue gaze touched her hair, her body beneath the silk and the length of her legs.

Embarrassed, uncertain, Lorrie moved to the other side of the bed and slid her legs beneath the sheet.

"Lorraine," he said and she looked at him. "I know we're young."

She studied his dark hair, his handsome jaw and expressive mouth.

"But we're going to be very happy together," he promised. He took her hand in both of his and reverently brushed his fingers over the back. "All I want is to make you happy."

The sincerity in his eyes caught her breath. How could she be so fortunate? Yes, their fathers had pushed them together in the beginning, but they had fallen in love of their own accord. To see love in this man's eyes filled her with hope and happiness. "I am happy," she replied sincerely.

"You're so lovely," he said and brushed her hair back with his fingers. "Can you believe we're really here? Alone together?"

A flutter of anxiety swelled in her breast. She loved him. That first time had been hurried and uncomfortable, and she'd tried to overcome the sense of disappointment. Was there something wrong with her? Would he think so?

"I want to please you, Lorraine," he said softly. "I want you to be comfortable in telling me what you want and what you like. Okay?"

"I—I don't know," she said, warmth rising up her neck and cheeks. What did he want her to say?

He scooted closer, stretching his long form the length of the bed, and kissed her.

The touch of his lips demanded nothing but her full attention. Warm and pliant, they spoke words of wonder and discovery. Since their engagement, he'd kissed her chastely, holding himself back, as if he was waiting for this moment. His kisses had always been pleasant, but this one...this one surpassed pleasant, zinged right past it and headed for exquisite. He cupped her face, tilted his face and adored her with his mouth.

Lorrie inhaled with surprise.

"What's wrong?" he said against her lips.

"Nothing...nothing..." She laid her hand on his shoulder.

"What?"

"It's just that . . . you've never kissed me like that."

Beneath her fingers, his shoulder tensed.

"I liked it," she admitted.

He relaxed again. "I've never been your husband before," he said.

"No. No, you haven't." This close, his eyes were deep blue pools of passion and concern.

She kissed him this time, wrapping her arms around his neck so that he enfolded her in his arms. He lowered their bodies flat on the bed. When his tongue touched her lips, it was a query, not an invasion.

Lorrie parted her lips and welcomed him, wonderingly enjoying the unrushed build of excitement that shimmered through her body at the sweet thrust and parry of their tongues.

He lowered a hand, pulled the sheet away and cupped her buttocks, bringing her against him, showing her how badly he wanted her, needed her. The display, through his clothing and her nightclothes, excited her unexplainably. She ran her free hand over his chest through his shirt, slid her fingers beneath his collar and caressed his warm neck, fanned her hand along his jaw.

"Lorraine," he groaned, pressing his face into her palm, burning her skin with his lips and tongue.

"Tom," she'd whispered. His mouth had stilled on her palm, his fingers sliding around her wrist and pulling her hand away.

What had she done?

The bedroom door opened and closed, jarring Lorraine back to the present. The room had grown completely dark while she'd been absorbed in memories of that night so long ago.

Quietly, Dan used the bathroom, turning the light on and off while the door was shut so as not to disturb her.

She realized she hadn't even undressed, hadn't gotten under the covers. He slid between the sheets several feet from her. She barely felt the mattress move. It was an enormous bed with plenty of room between them for all their pain and disappointments.

How could she not have known?

Chapter 5

Lorraine lay still, pretending she was asleep. A cool breeze drifted in through the sliding screen door she'd left open. She couldn't remember a time before in their marriage that she'd pretended anything with him. If she was awake when he came to bed, she always snuggled up against him.

She'd never had to pretend. About anything.

"Tom?" she'd said that night in the hotel. "Is something wrong?"

A hurt look had crossed his features, followed by an expression almost like resignation or a measured decision. A sudden fear had gripped her and she'd pulled back.

"Lorraine, nothing is wrong," he'd said.

She couldn't make herself meet his eyes. "Did you do this just to please your father? If I thought you'd married me only for our fathers, I'd . . . I'd die."

One hand firmly turned her face up to his. "No.
Don't ever think that again. I married you because I've
never wanted anything in my life more than I want to be
with you. I married you because I love you."

However unexpected, his words were so sincere, so
direct, she couldn't doubt them. "Promise?"

He placed her hand over his heart. "I promise. I'll
prove how much I love you. I'll get rid of any doubt you
ever had."

And he had.

He kissed her with affection and intensity and un-
swerving ardency. He touched her through her clothing, setting her newborn passion aflame. He removed
her wrapper and gown, the expression on his face only
describable as awe. "You're so beautiful, I never
knew."

No, before they hadn't had time or opportunity for a
leisurely perusal of each other's bodies. Lorrie hadn't
known, as she did now when he shrugged out of his
shirt, that the sight of his muscled chest and arms could
send a tingle of anticipation from her breasts to her abdomen and lower. She hadn't imagined that his bare
hips, his long legs and rigid arousal would entice her
hands to explore his supple flesh and learn the wonders
of his male body.

"I never knew, either," she whispered against his
chest.

His hands covered her breasts with worshipful attention, stroked her skin in so many places, she marveled
at his devoted attention. He kissed her hands, her feet,
the sensitive spots behind her knees, the juncture of her
thighs, the column of her neck, her lips, her breasts.

"Don't make me wait any longer," she heard herself
beg.

He smiled, a drugged smile of passion and pleasure. "Always tell me what you need," he said.

"I need you," she replied without awkwardness. He wouldn't allow her embarrassment or hesitation.

"This is our promise," he said, lowering his body over hers. "This seals our vows. Now you're mine."

She touched his cheek and opened to him. "And you're mine."

He led himself to her, to the very edge of entry, and paused, locking their fingers, palm to palm, and gazing into her eyes with engulfing intensity. "I love you, Lorraine."

A thrill of pleasure warmed her. He'd never said those words before. Marriage had brought out a whole new side of him she'd only dared to hope for. She couldn't reply around the emotion in her throat.

She hadn't expected the rush of sensation and the spiraling mixture of delight and agony that shimmered through her when he pushed into her and began a graceful rhythm. Delight that it was so much better than she remembered or dreamed, and an agony of pent-up need that grew and spiraled and intensified until she couldn't breathe or speak or feel anything but his damp, hair-roughened skin, the glide of his sex against the very core of her being, and his mouth on her breasts.

Lorraine burst against him in wondrous release, gripping his hair with her fingers, and straining her body to receive as much of him as he could give. A series of gasps escaped her lips, and a quick rush of tears followed.

He spent himself inside her, against her, around her, enfolding her in his embrace and kissing the moisture from her lashes.

"Always remember I love you," he'd said on a ragged breath. "Always."

Lorrie blinked, and realized the tears on her cheeks were real, not a memory. On the other side of the bed, a million miles away, Dan lay unmoving. Was he asleep? Silently, she got up, removed her damp, wrinkled clothing and slipped a nightgown over her head.

If only she could be sure he was asleep, she'd move over there against him. Comfort herself with his warmth and nearness. *Always remember I love you,* he'd said.

Could that love still assure her? Comfort her? Was its meaning lost to her now?

That's why she cried. That's why anger and hurt warred within her—because so much was lost to her. And, Lord help her, she wanted it back. But she feared she wanted the impossible.

Dan slept for a fitful hour, only to wake up unable to go back to sleep. He grabbed a pair of jeans and slipped into the hall. At least she'd agreed not to send him away from their room. At least . . .

At least they had the pretense of a real marriage.

He wandered out to the tractor barn and watched a pair of headlights travel the long drive from the house to the road. His Dad and Tom were getting home awfully late. The garage door opened and closed and a minute later the kitchen light went on. About twenty minutes passed and the light went out, replaced by one in the family room, which was quickly doused. They'd had a snack and gone to bed.

He walked through the fragrant freshly mowed grass to the edge of the meadow behind the house and sat. Their bedroom windows were open, as well as the slid-

ing glass doors. She could hear him through the screens
if he called out.

Was she sleeping?

A dull ache throbbed from behind his dry eyes into
the front of his skull. The light turned off in Gil's upstairs room.

What would he do when he found out? Would Lorraine tell him? Somehow, Dan didn't think so. It would
be up to him.

The house had been so quiet without the children.
Evenings without them were few and far between, and
usually, Dan and Lorraine used the rare opportunities
to their fullest. In the darkness, he made out the cushioned furniture on the deck outside their bedroom.
More than once they'd made love on the chaise longue.

His gaze followed the stairs down to the above-
ground pool. A couple of times they'd used the time
alone to skinny-dip. The memories sliced his already
ragged heart deeper. What was the worst that could
happen?

They could go on living like this. They would never
be a couple again, sleeping on separate sides of the bed.

She could leave him.

She could want Tom.

What would all of this do to their kids?

Lorraine appeared at the full-length screen, her long
nightgown illuminated by the moonlight. The breeze
caught the whispery fabric and sucked it against the
screen, then blew it back against her body, forward and
back. With one hand, she lifted the hair from her neck
and held it on the back of her head, leaning her elbow
against the door frame and standing that way, her
nightgown billowing back and forth.

She couldn't see him down here. She wouldn't think to look for him at the edge of the yard in the night.

Dan strained his already aching eyes in the blackness, trying to make out her face, her satiny neck, the slope of her breasts, the curve of her hip. He couldn't see her feet, but he knew the way she stood with one foot atop the other, her dainty pink toes curled and her knee pointing seductively.

He'd never told her how sexy that was.

At last she moved away, and he released a pent-up breath, not knowing he'd been holding it.

There were a lot of things he'd never told her. He wanted to touch her, to hold her, to tell her he was sorry and that she meant everything to him. But his love didn't mean much to her now. His love had been a selfish love. His love had only ended up hurting her.

Lorraine was grateful the kids weren't home. She'd overslept and awakened with a start. She took a cool shower, hoping to revive herself.

It wasn't unusual for her to put on makeup when they went somewhere, so she applied foundation and added gloss to her lips. She didn't know if she'd be going to pick up the kids from her mother's or not, but after the night she'd just spent, she needed the concealing makeup.

Dressed in shorts and a sleeveless top, she opened the hamper and reached in. Beneath her nightgown lay his jeans and T-shirt. Lorrie couldn't stop her hand. It went directly to his cotton shirt and lifted it to her nose.

That outdoorsy smell assailed her, a little like fresh air and a full day's work. A lot like man. Tears smarted behind her scratchy lids and she buried the garment deep in the pile of laundry and carried it downstairs.

Tom was fixing breakfast with his one good arm. Gil sat at the table, and *Dan* stood staring out the back door with a mug of coffee in his hand.

"Mornin', Lorrie," Gil said.

"Morning." She hurried toward the laundry room.

"Seems strange without the kids, doesn't it?" her father-in-law called after her.

She sensed Dan's eyes following her, but she couldn't look. She mumbled a reply and automatically sorted the laundry, jamming his T-shirt into the washer and running hot water on it.

"I'll come in around eleven and we'll go get the kids," he said from behind her.

She nodded. A minute later, she turned and he was gone.

Tom sat a plate at her place and motioned with the metal spatula. Lorrie slid onto her chair and noted the fried egg with crispy brown edges.

"Here." Gil pushed buttered slices of overdone toast toward her.

"Thanks."

The three of them ate together, and Lorrie stole glances at the man she now knew was Thomas. The man she'd wanted to marry. He tried to dunk his toast in the well-done egg, and settled for cutting a piece and laying it on top before he bit it. The man she'd had sex with in the back of her father's Buick.

Lorrie's bite of egg stuck in her throat. She washed it down with bitterly strong coffee. Tom glanced up. He smiled.

Lorrie returned an embarrassed half smile. He'd had his hair cut the day before, the shorter style and now-revealed silver at his temples emphasizing the brothers' likeness. His skin wasn't as dark. He didn't eat like Dan. He had that little scar on his chin.

He looked at her again and she stared back. There was a difference. Something about the set of his eyes that was unlike Dan. And his mouth...

"Want another egg?" he asked.

"No, this is fine, thanks."

A red Nebraska cap with a black bill hung on the chair post behind his shoulder. Tom had always liked ball caps. How come she hadn't noticed when the man she'd married had preferred a Stetson?

Gil ate his breakfast, blissfully unaware of any change of identity or roiling turmoil in the Beckett household. How could he not have realized Tom was the son who left? Why hadn't he seen the subtle differences in his sons? Dan could tell their sons apart in a heartbeat.

Because Gil had wanted to believe Tom had stayed and changed. Just as she had. How it must have hurt Dan to know that.

She realized Tom had stopped eating and was holding his fork above his plate. Gil noticed, too, and cocked his head. "Dan, you all right?"

Tom blinked and focused on his father. "The strangest thing just went through my head."

"What?" Gil asked.

"I had a picture of eating breakfast with you, but it wasn't this kitchen. The table was one of those old round pedestal types and there was a metal cart full of plants in front of the window."

"That was the old house. The kitchen at the old house," Gil said excitedly. "What else?"

"That's all. That just came to me and nothing more."

Gil grinned and turned to Lorrie. "He just described the old place, didn't he?"

She nodded.

"Your mother loved houseplants," Gil went on. "She had 'em all over the house. Lorrie kept 'em alive for years."

"The philodendron in the family room was hers," Lorrie added, trying to sound natural.

As the two men continued their meal, unease crept over her. That little snippet of the past meant Tom's memories were in there somewhere. Dan had been right in worrying that Tom's ability to recall them would come back and throw their lives into chaos.

She finished eating without tasting a bite, loaded the plates and silverware into the dishwasher, and quickly scrubbed the skillet. Her father-in-law and brother-in-law wandered off. She had a couple of loads of laundry folded by the time the back door opened and closed.

"Let me grab a quick shower and we'll go."

She could smell him. Sunny air and freshly mowed grass, the masculine scent that clung to his clothing. Without turning from the potatoes she was slicing into a casserole dish for that night's supper, she nodded.

Just before he returned, she found a pair of sandals in the pile of footwear just inside the laundry room and strapped them on. She grabbed her purse, slung the strap over her shoulder, and walked ahead of him through to the garage.

Behind her, Dan hit the button for the garage-door opener, while she slid into the passenger seat of their Explorer.

He climbed in on the driver's side and automatically fastened his seat belt. Lorrie did the same, the clicks loud in the enclosed space. He didn't move to start the engine, and she stared ahead, through the opening, at the sunny drive.

Silence closed in around them. Lorrie's heart beat in a slow, painful rhythm.

"Lorraine, are you all right?"

Her heart thudded. His voice sounded exactly as it always had. He smelled the same—like soap and freshly washed cotton. If she turned her head he would even look the same.

But he wasn't. He wasn't Tom. He was her husband, her lover, but he wasn't Tom.

"Lorr—"

"I'm as all right as can be expected, I guess."

Several seconds passed. "Will you look at me?"

What did he want from her? What did he expect of her? She prepared her heart and turned her head.

The brim of his Stetson didn't hide the pain and regret in his tortured blue eyes. He hadn't slept well either. The Navajo print shirt she'd bought him for Father's Day was tucked into the waistband of his jeans, molding his chest, and he'd rolled the sleeves back over his forearms.

This was the man she'd lived with. The man she'd loved. The man who'd given her children and built them a house. This was Dan. And he was a stranger.

He had no words of reassurance to offer her. What could he have said? She turned away and he started the engine. They didn't speak all the way to Nebraska City.

Lorrie's mother, Ruby Loring, had prepared a Sunday lunch for all of them. She was a lovely woman who didn't look her age, the fact no doubt helped considerably by her trips to the beauty salon to keep her hair the same nutmeg color as Lorrie's.

Autumn and the twins hauled their father off to the picket-fenced side yard where they had the chipped and scarred croquet set arranged.

Thad and Orrin Loring had a chess game underway on the back porch. Lorrie watched them for a few minutes. Her father and Gil had known each other for years. They'd been involved with the American Legion post since Lorrie could remember. Orrin had always taken her to the pancake feeds and fish fries. In fact, that's where'd she'd first met Tom.

Tom hadn't given her the time of day until high school, and then she'd wondered if it was only at the insistence of his father that he'd asked her out.

Orrin had bragged up Tom and encouraged her to see him. He'd never really said much about Tom's brother running off and he'd bestowed a generous check upon them as a wedding gift. What would he think if she told him that man out there in the yard wasn't Tom, after all?

Shrugging off the thought, she went in and helped her mom with the dishes.

"You look awfully tired," Ruby commented, moving past her daughter to wipe the table. "If I didn't know better, I'd think you were pregnant again."

"I didn't sleep very well last night," she said.

"The kids stayed here, so you had to make the most of your night, eh?" her mother said with a wry grin.

"Something like that."

Ruby hung the dishcloth over the sink divider and her expression turned serious. "Hon, are you okay?"

Lorrie nodded.

"You know I'm here if you want to talk."

She nodded again.

Ruby moved forward and held her in a floral-scented hug. Lorrie's eyes smarted and she clung to her mother for a minute, fighting back the tears and the overpowering sense that her life was spinning out of control. She wished she could talk to someone about this. But she couldn't. Not yet. Not until she had things sorted out in her mind and was able to put a little objectivity into her thinking.

"I'm just tired, Mom."

"I'll pick you up a B complex when I shop," Ruby offered. "Have you been taking your multivitamins?"

Lorrie pulled back and actually grinned. "You're such a mom."

Lorrie's sister Lorna arrived, along with her husband and daughter, and the afternoon turned into evening. Dan and Lorrie herded their family into the Explorer.

Having the kids with them made the trip home seem almost normal. Bram and Jori bickered and Dan had to stop and assign them different seats. Autumn bubbled on and on about the nest of baby finches in Grandma's hanging begonia, and Thad thumped a rhythm on the back of Dan's seat while he listened to music through his headphones.

If it hadn't been for the sick, empty feeling that gouged Lorrie's heart every time she happened to glance at Dan, things might have seemed ordinary.

But it was there between them. A chasm as deep and wide as any earthquake could create. A transgression with no solution, no answers, no end.

Supper time seemed normal.

"Will you swim with me when it's dark tonight, Daddy?" Autumn asked.

"It's too late for you once it's dark," Dan replied.

Her lower lip stuck out.

"How about if I swim with you after supper?" he asked.

Her cherubic face brightened. "Yes! Will you play *Free Willy* with me?"

"Which one of us is Willy?" he asked.

"You, silly," she replied.

"I thought so." He grinned and ruffled her bangs.

"We're getting plenty of sun these days," Gil said.

Dan agreed. "The crop looks good."

"Looks like spraying helped, too," his father said.

Dan nodded.

After the family had eaten, Lorraine placed the leftover cakes in the center of the table. "We'll have to slice these narrow to make it go around."

"None for me," Gil said, pushing his plate back.

Automatically, Tom sliced himself a chunk of the lemon chiffon and balanced it on the knife to his plate. He took a bite.

"What're you doin' eatin' Tom's cake?" Gil asked.

Tom looked up, fork poised. "I wanted a slice of this one. Anything wrong with that?"

Dan and Lorraine exchanged an uncomfortable glance and he saw a wave of realization pass over her expression. "Nothing wrong with that," she hurried to say. "You can eat any kind you want."

"He never used to like lemon," Gil grumbled.

"People can change," Lorraine said. "There are a lot of things I didn't eat when I was a kid that I like now."

Deliberately, she sliced a piece of the chocolate and placed it in front of Dan.

He stared at it for seconds, wondering what the gesture meant. A funny feeling settled in his chest. She was acknowledging who he was. She had protected the secret by defending Tom wanting a slice of the other cake. He looked up, but she was serving the kids and didn't meet his eyes.

He pierced a forkful of cake and brought it to his mouth, barely tasting it. With obvious relish, Tom polished off his slice in no time. Little by little, Tom's personality was being revealed. Uneasily, Dan glanced at his father, but he'd refilled his coffee mug and was placidly stirring his sweetener in. He still didn't have a clue.

"I gotta get my swimming suit on." Autumn hopped down and picked up her battered box of crayons and a Barney coloring book she'd left on the counter. Before disappearing into the family room, she gave Dan a flirtatious grin and waved with a flip of her hand beneath the book.

Dan winked. "Meet you at the pool."

"Dad?"

Dan focused his attention on Thad. He had a strange haircut this summer, practically shaved on the sides and long on top. Dan didn't much care for it, but remembered the wild things teens had been doing with their hair when he was in high school and decided it was pretty tame.

"Remember that talk we had about me working at the Kenneys' truck garden?" Thad asked.

Dan nodded. "I talked with Mr. Kenney. Is that what you want to do?"

"Not really." Thad shrugged. "It's too far to drive all the time until I can drive myself. It can wait another year or so."

Pride welled up in Dan's chest. "That's really mature of you, Thad."

He shrugged. "Yeah, well, it would mean a lot of evenings, too, and I wanna play softball."

Dan resisted grinning. "We start picking the north orchards tomorrow. I'll give you a raise for picking and for the Festival."

"Cool." Thad got up and started to leave the kitchen.

"Thad." Lorraine called in a singsongy voice. "It's your night to help with dishes."

"Can't I do 'em later?" he asked, turning back.

Lorraine gave Dan a pointed look. Such a normal situation. "Do them now, son," Dan said gently.

The words slipped out naturally. Lorraine's hands stilled on the plates she'd been stacking. She looked up and their eyes met.

They hadn't discussed it.

When had she realized that Thad wasn't his son, Dan wondered. Yesterday? Just now?

Dan fled upstairs to get his trunks on.

Chapter 6

Somehow Lorraine had made it through the afternoon, through supper, through the evening. She tucked Autumn, smelling like Mr. Bubble, into bed and kissed her soft, shiny cheek with a sweet sadness she could barely endure.

"Where's Daddy?"

"He'll be here. He always tucks you in."

Autumn nodded. "Daddy is a great Willy."

"Daddy's pretty good at everything, isn't he?"

Her daughter nodded solemnly. "I had a fun day. I had a fun night at Gramma's last night, too, but I did miss you guys a teeny bit."

"I missed you, too."

"Me an' Bram and Jori slept in your old room, and Thad slept on the back porch. I worried a bear would get him."

"There aren't any bears in Nebraska, darlin'."

"Uh-huh, at the zoo."

"Yes, at the zoo, but they're very careful not to let the animals get loose."

"Good. 'Night, Mama."

"'Night, darlin'." She left the night-light softly glowing and the door open. She remembered the very real fears of childhood. Worries of Godzilla or King Kong thrashing through her town. Fears of unknown things under her bed at night. All so ungrounded in reality, and yet so painfully real.

Thank goodness children had no concept of the real terrors waiting in life.

Lorrie closed herself behind her bedroom door and surveyed the spacious room. She opened and closed Dan's drawers and looked in his closet. The cowboy hat he'd bought in Texas sat, brim up, wrapped in tissue paper on the top shelf. It was his dress-up hat, one he'd seldom worn, purchased during their vacation to Fort Worth and Dallas.

Everything reminded her of some part of their life together. He was everywhere in this room. In this house.

Lorrie undressed, put on a nightshirt, sat on the bed's edge, and realized something. She was thinking about her husband as if he were dead.

And he was. The husband she'd thought she had didn't exist. Had never existed. She was grieving, and she had a right to her grief.

She heard his voice down the hall as he spoke to the boys and wished Autumn a good night. A nervous unease rippled in her chest. The way he'd looked at her after supper, after calling his son "son" had torn at her. Did he deserve all the guilt she'd seen behind his guarded expression? She had to tell him.

He didn't come to their room. He must have gone to his office where he sometimes did paperwork or stud-

ied or worked on his hybrid projects in the evenings.
The house grew silent. Lorrie turned on the bedside
lamp and tried to read the same novel she'd been reading for two weeks. She couldn't concentrate. She
couldn't relate to the silly story, anyway. The fictional
couple would eventually work out all their problems
and live happily ever after.

She opened the drawer of her nightstand and chucked
the book inside, slamming the drawer and reaching for
the remote control. She ended up watching a rerun of
Coach, Dan's favorite. He always laughed out loud at
Luther's antics.

Laughter erupted from the television and she realized she hadn't heard a bit of the dialogue. The door
opened, surprising her.

Dan went into the bathroom. While the shower ran,
her heart tripped doubletime. *Showtime.* How had he
lived all those years with that secret eating away inside
him? She couldn't bear the way it felt to keep the truth
about Thad to herself now that she knew Dan's pain.

He appeared in a pair of jogging shorts, his dark hair
towel-dried and combed back. She watched a commercial for a long-distance company. He climbed into his
side of the bed.

Several minutes passed while the program finished
and the credits ran. "When did you realize?" he asked.
"About Thad, I mean."

Her heart slammed against her ribs. Why did she care
if he hated her? He'd hurt her this much, why did she
care if he hurt, too? "I thought about it yesterday," she
said.

"It never made any difference to me," he said, his
voice sounding choked. "But now...now I think it's not
fair to Tom. Maybe he should know—"

"No!" She said the word automatically—vehemently.

Dan looked at her in surprise. "Have you thought about it?"

She pointed the remote and turned the volume down. "Of course I've thought about it."

"Well, did you think that maybe Tom deserves to know he has a son? It would kill me to lose that—" he gestured with one hand "—connection we have. I've been a father to him since he was born. But what I did wasn't fair to a lot of people. Especially you."

The sorrow in his words ate at her. The confession soured on the end of her tongue, waiting for her to garner courage. Seconds passed.

"So you don't want me to tell him?" he asked.

She phrased it a dozen different ways in her mind.

"Lorraine?"

"Tom doesn't have a son." There, she'd blurted it out. She couldn't seem to get enough air to fill her lungs.

"What?"

She couldn't look him in the eye. Staring at his bare chest wasn't comfortable, either. She focused on the lampshade. "There's something you don't know. I never told you because—well, I guess I didn't want you to think I'd trapped you into proposing to me. I really believed I was pregnant. That night when I came and told you, I thought for sure I was. You asked me to marry you, and everything was going so well... We were happy...."

In her peripheral vision, he didn't move a muscle.

"The next week I got my period."

The muted television in the background was the only sound.

"I didn't tell you. The wedding was planned, our parents were going along with it, you were—I thought you had somehow changed and..." Lorraine fidgeted with the hem of the sheet. "Well, anyway, I didn't have another period. I got pregnant with Thad right away. It didn't seem to make any difference then. We were happy." Finally, she turned her gaze to his face. "Do you know what I'm saying?"

His lips moved before he spoke, and finally the words came out—quietly—almost fearfully. "Thad is my son?"

She nodded.

His eyes glistened. He leaned forward with his elbows on his knees and covered his face with his hands. Lorraine reached for his bare shoulder, but drew her hand back before she touched him. Tears trickled down her own cheeks and she wiped them on the sheet.

Without warning, he threw back the covers, crossed to open the sliding doors and disappeared outside.

Lorraine couldn't bear the sense of loss, the fear of what their combined deception had cost. As confused as he'd made her, she was miserable without him. She waited a few minutes before she followed.

He stood with both hands braced on the wood railing, his face tipped to the heavens, moonlight defining the planes and hollows of his muscled torso. Below them the sound of the pool filter gurgled steadily.

She wanted nothing more than to step behind him, press her cheek to the warm flesh of his back and give him comfort, draw comfort. She had to hold her hands at her sides and stop three feet away.

"Not telling you was a betrayal," she admitted. "I see that now. I don't expect you to forgive me, but I needed to tell you."

He turned his head and shoulders toward her. "A betrayal? I guess so. But telling me tonight was a gift. Thank you," he whispered.

An ache yawned in her chest. Lord, the man was a saint! His acceptance and forgiveness made her feel more than ever like a heel. How could he deal with something like this in a matter of minutes? It seemed she'd been confused and hurting forever. "Couldn't you get mad?" she asked. "Couldn't you call me a conniving little bitch and throw something?"

She threaded her fingers into her hair and stared at him.

"Do you think that would make you feel better?" he asked. "Trust me, it doesn't."

"Maybe," she said, dropping her hand and slapping her thigh. "Maybe it would. Maybe I wouldn't have to feel like the only one who has trouble dealing with deception."

"There's a big difference," he said. "You've just told me that the boy I love with all my heart, and thought was Tom's, is my own son. This is one less complication I have to regret and deal with."

"But ever since I found out you were Dan, I let you think he wasn't your child!"

"You're right. It hurts like hell. But I'm certainly the last person to condemn someone for not telling the truth."

She dropped onto one of the cushioned redwood chairs. "You're not a very good fighter," she accused. "You never have been."

It was a familiar lament. One he'd always replied to with, "No, but I'm a hell of a lover," and she'd had no recourse but to agree and laugh and make him prove it.

The reminder of their history together hung in the air like the heat and humidity of the September night.

He went in.

Twenty minutes later, she followed and slid into bed, lying still, and feeling more alone than she'd ever known was possible. Sometime before sleep claimed her, the warmth of his legs touched hers. She only had to turn a little to curl her body against his. Neither of them spoke and she wasn't even sure he was awake. Feeling better than she had in days, she closed her eyes and drifted into sleep.

A long, tiring week followed. Gil taught Tom how to sort, a task that the two could handle together, considering Gil's limited stamina and Tom's one good arm. The itinerant workers showed up and worked hard. The college students that Dan had hired were good workers, pleasant around the children, and on Saturday they promised to be back early Monday morning to help work the last section.

Gil wasn't a very intuitive person. That's why his covert glances and occasional queries about Lorraine bothered Dan. If Gil had noticed the strain, how was all of this affecting the children?

The children. An enormous weight had been lifted from Dan's heart. His children. All of them. On Sunday afternoon, the family relaxed by picnicking and playing softball in the side yard. Dan missed balls, struck out time and again, and just couldn't seem to pay attention. He finally had time to look at Thad, watch him play, admire his youthful energy and his handsome features.

Knowing Thad was his own was like seeing him for the first time. He was caught up in the wonder of it.

After Thad hit a home run, Dan hugged him hard and didn't let go. "I love you, son," he said, holding him by the shoulders and looking him in the eye.

"Heck, I know that, Dad," Thad said, shrugging out of his hold. "You don't have to get all mushy."

"Right. Sorry." He turned his faded green-and-yellow DEKALB cap backward and threw himself into the game.

When Tom took a turn at bat they gave him a handicap by being one-handed outfielders. He got to third base anyway; he'd always been a great ballplayer.

"When are we gonna swim?" Autumn begged. She'd tired of the ball game quickly and sat on the side of the field with Gil.

Dan glanced over. They'd put her off most of the afternoon. "How about after this inning we cool off in the pool before supper?"

The others agreed.

Autumn squealed as the boys carried the bats and gloves to the garage. "Yippee! Who's gonna be Willy?"

"Isn't it Bram's turn to be Willy?" Dan asked.

Bram groaned and Jori elbowed him in the ribs. A tussle broke out and they chased each other into the house.

Dressed in suits and carrying towels, the family reunited on the deck. The sun had warmed the water, but it was still refreshing. Gil and Tom watched from the shaded portion of the deck.

"Watch me!" Autumn cried repeatedly, jumping in and swimming back to the ladder.

Lorrie seated herself on the side with the sun warming her back, and watched her daughter's antics. Dan indulged Autumn, pretending surprise when she jumped in and splashed him ten times in a row.

The boys started their favorite whirlpool game, circling the perimeter so fast that water splashed over the sides through the deck. Usually by the time they were finished, the pool needed a couple of feet added. Autumn hated it, because she couldn't keep her head above the turbulence.

Dan let them continue a while and then called, "Come on, fellas. Let's go throw some supper together."

"Aw!"

"Oh, man!"

The three of them groaned, but Dan herded them out through the gate.

"There's cold chicken and a couple of melons," Lorrie offered.

"Gotcha." Dan disappeared after the boys.

Lorrie enjoyed the sun a while longer, lazily watching Autumn jump and splash. Finally, she knew the guys would have the food ready, and she urged Autumn out of the water and toward the front.

A car door slammed and Lorrie rounded the corner, skirting the unfamiliar burgundy Taurus parked in the drive. She towel-dried her hair and slung the damp towel over her shoulder as they approached the back door.

A feminine squeal erupted from the kitchen. Mother and daughter exchanged a perplexed glance and Autumn ran forward and yanked the door open. Lorrie followed.

And stopped dead in her tracks just inside.

A young woman with short black hair had her pale arms around Dan's neck, holding him to her for a full-fledged mouth-to-mouth, eyes-closed kiss! Dan, still dressed in his trunks with his hair finger-slicked back, gingerly rested his fingertips at the waistband of her shorts.

Bram and Jori had never stood so close together without jostling or arguing. They, too, stared, dishes and silverware forgotten in their hands.

Thad had turned from the counter and watched the encounter with his brows knotted in the middle of his forehead.

A feeling like nothing Lorrie had ever known welled up inside her at the sight of her husband kissing another woman. Staring, she moved a little closer to see if Dan's eyes were closed, too.

The slender woman drew back and framed Dan's face in her palms. "Oh, Buzz!" she squealed.

To his credit, Dan's fingers went to her wrists and pulled her hands from his face. A blush Lorrie'd seldom seen darkened his tan considerably.

"Daddy?" Autumn questioned.

Dan turned to Lorrie and his daughter and immediately backed away from the affectionate young woman.

Lorrie said nothing. She hadn't spoken his name since he'd told her the truth and neither name came naturally to her lips.

The dark-haired woman turned wide brown eyes on Lorrie, then glanced around at the rest of her audience. "Hi, guys."

She stood uncomfortably beside Dan, obviously expecting a reaction and looking as if she wanted to climb Dan's frame. Impatiently, she straightened her posture and absently combed her fingers through the wispy hair on her neck.

"I'm Cedra." She stepped forward and reached for Lorrie's hand. "Cedra Chaney. I'm a friend of Buzz's," she said with a soft drawl. She moved back beside Dan as if she didn't want to get too far away. Her short haircut gave her a pixieish appearance, cute and endearing in a bold sort of way. "I was beside myself when he disappeared. Just this week, I traced him to the hospital in Trousdale and talked with Dr. Vance."

Lorrie met Dan's eyes briefly, his registering as much confusion as she knew hers must. This girl thought Dan was Tom—no big surprise.

Cedra turned her attention back to Dan. "I had to tell him I was your wife before he'd tell me you couldn't remember anything, and that your family came and identified you as Daniel Beckett. He gave me your address and phone number. I didn't call. I'm sorry. I was in a hurry to see you." She frowned worriedly at Lorrie and then at Dan. "You're not—married, are you?"

"Cedra—" Dan began.

"Do you remember me?" she asked.

"Sit down," he said, kindly, gesturing to a wooden chair.

"No, just tell me."

"I'm not who you think I am," he explained. "You must have known my brother—"

"Supper ready?" The voice came from the family room, and they all turned to see Tom and Gil come through the doorway and stop.

Cedra Chaney's dark brown eyes opened wide in disbelief and surprise. She stared at Tom and then back to Dan and looked back again. From her pale face and shocked expression, Lorraine worried that she might faint. But the girl was obviously made of sterner stuff than she'd given her credit for, and accepted the mirror image of the man she'd just kissed silly with a shake of her head. "*You're* Buzz?" she asked.

Everyone stared at Tom. Did he know this girl? Would seeing her provoke his memory?

"You know me?" Tom asked.

She glanced from one brother to another. "Were you living in Missouri and Tennessee the last couple of years?"

"Wasn't him," Tom said with a nod at his brother. "Must be me."

Cedra gave Dan an apologetic glance, hurried over to Tom and slid her arm beneath his good one. "I'm Cedra."

"Hi," Tom said and studied her face near his shoulder.

"Thad, get another plate," Dan instructed. Just like that, Cedra was invited for supper. What else could he have done, Lorrie thought. The kids were hungry, the food was ready. She'd been too surprised to think of it herself.

"Run on up and put dry clothes on, sweetie," Lorrie told Autumn. Seconds later, she hurried into their bathroom and pulled her suit off and dried her cold skin. Grabbing a comb, she ran it through her tangled hair and dabbed on a little lipstick.

"Suddenly everyone's dressing for dinner." Dan's voice from the bedroom startled her. She pulled a towel around herself and padded across the carpet to her chest of drawers.

"Can't sit around the table in our wet suits with company here."

"You didn't mind me inviting her?" Dan questioned.

"There really wasn't much choice," she replied, slipping into her underclothes, a pair of shorts and a T-shirt

as they spoke. "She obviously knows Tom and was relieved to see that he was all right."

"Very relieved." She heard the sound of Dan's jeans
zipping and turned.

He stood in front of his bureau strapping on his
wristwatch, and looked up. Lorrie stepped over and
used the corner of her damp towel to rub away the fus-
chia lipstick smeared across his lips. Their eyes met.

Lorrie lowered the towel. It had been a good many
years since either of them had kissed another person.
"Was she a good kisser?"

The corner of his mouth quirked up in amusement.
"She's all right."

She stuffed the towel into his hands and left the
room.

Lorraine's reaction to that mistaken kiss pleased Dan
in a big way. She was jealous.

Cedra was the main attraction at dinner. She seated
herself beside Tom and babied him, placing food on his
plate, cutting his chicken. "You poor thing," she said
with her lips pooched out in a silly fashion. "Now that
I'm here, you won't have to want for *any*thing."

Tom's expression didn't exactly reveal horror at the
idea, and the sexual implication was blatant. Even the
boys elbowed one another and grinned. Gil ate his supper without looking up.

"So, where are you from?" Lorraine asked Cedra in
an attempt at polite conversation.

"We were living in Clarksville," she replied. "We
have an apartment with a deck and a pool." She turned
back to Tom. "Do you remember the pool, swee-
tums?" She batted her silky black lashes.

"I don't remember anything," Tom answered.

Displeasure furrowed her brow. "Oh. Well, it's on Jenkins Avenue. You work at Nick's Cycle Emporium and I tend bar at Rocking Em's. We hang out there on the weekends, you know, play sand volleyball and darts and all that."

Dan tried not to raise his eyebrows at this revelation of his brother's life. It all sounded so alien. His father never even looked up.

"That's just been for about the last year and a half," she explained. "You said you'd been in Missouri before that."

"What did he do at the Cycle Emporium?" Dan couldn't resist asking.

"Buzz does custom bikes. Awesome work. Ever seen his Harley?"

Dan couldn't help the surprise he felt. Tom working on cycles! That was too ironic! "Yeah, it's in the tractor barn, looking like it went through a trash compactor."

"Oh, you poor baby!" Cedra exclaimed and patted Tom's arm. "It meant so much to you."

Tom shrugged offhandedly, as if he didn't remember the Harley having any special meaning.

She snuggled up and kissed the underside of his jaw. "When your arm's all better you can fix your bike. I'll help you. I'll do whatever you need—run for parts, hand you stuff. Won't that be great?"

The children had finished their food, but sat listening in rapt attention.

"Why don't you kids go watch a video until bedtime," Lorraine suggested.

Jori stood and picked up his plate. "We'll help with the dishes."

"Yeah," agreed Bram who had never in his lifetime agreed with his brother on anything that Lorrie could remember, and the two of them usually fought over whose night it was to do dishes.

She cocked a brow at her sons, letting them know they weren't putting anything over on her. "I'll do the dishes tonight. You watch a movie. Something suitable for Autumn," she warned.

Knowing better than to grumble in front of the guest, the four excused themselves and headed for the family room.

Lorraine made a pot of coffee and poured it into mugs for the adults seated around the table.

"Look, what's the deal here, anyway?" Cedra finally said with exasperation. "I've been living with this guy—" she gestured to Tom "—for a year, thinking he's Buzz Turner. One day he doesn't come home, I call the police, and after weeks, I finally get a lead at a hospital a couple hundred miles away, and I find out he's been identified as Daniel Beckett and brought here."

The Beckett family stared into their coffee mugs.

"Will someone please tell me what's going on?" she pleaded.

At last Dan spoke up. "He left home fourteen years ago. We hadn't seen him again until Dr. Vance called. He doesn't remember who he is right now, so he can't say why he was living as Buzz Turner."

"Turner's your ma's maiden name," Gil said, finally speaking.

"But he is going to remember, right?" she demanded. "He will remember who I am?" She turned and blinked up into Tom's eyes, tears spiking her lashes. "I want you to remember that you love me, Buzz."

Dan noted the tears that came to Lorraine's eyes at Cedra's despair. She sympathized with her frustration. No matter how unusual this woman was, she loved Tom, and was as confused by this situation as everyone else.

At least Dan didn't have to feel responsible for Cedra's heartache along with all the other guilt he was shouldering right now. Whatever Tom had been and done while he was gone was his own concern. And the accident was merely that—an accident. This new complication was not Dan's doing or his problem.

"It's as hard for me as it is for all of you," Tom said finally. "It's terrible to wake up inside a body I don't recognize, shave a face I've never seen before and meet people who say I should know them. You don't have to feel so damned insulted that I don't know who you are! *I* don't know who I am!" He struck his chest with his fist and stood.

That was the first time he'd spoken of his own frustration, though Dan had known it was there. He wondered if Tom shared his feelings with his counselor in the city.

"I'm sorry," Cedra said, standing beside him. "I am sorry. I was being selfish." She put her arms around him and laid her head on his chest, careful of his arm trapped between them.

Dan half expected Tom to push her away or stomp from the room. Instead, he rested his hand on her shoulder.

"What do you want me to call you?" she asked.

"Call me Buzz," he said with a sigh. "That's who I am to you. One name is as good as the next to me."

"It's going to be all right," she said. "I'll stay as long as it takes. Em gave me as much time as I needed away from my job. I'm going to be here for you."

Over her head, Tom looked at Dan. Dan looked at Gil, then over at Lorraine. She'd been running a finger around the rim of her cup, but she stopped and her eyes met Dan's.

Dan read the tired expression on her face without her speaking a word: *Criminy! What next?*

Chapter 7

Lorrie put the last glass in the dishwasher and turned to Cedra, the only person left in the kitchen. She'd obviously been distressed over Tom's disappearance. Her relief at finding him alive must have been diminished by his memory loss. Lorrie couldn't help but sympathize. "There's an extra twin bed in Autumn's room. You're welcome to sleep there."

Cedra's round, dark eyes reflected her frustration. She'd been sleeping with Tom for the past year, but he could hardly be expected to share a bed with a woman he didn't remember.

Besides, Lorraine thought, Tom slept on the sofa bed in the family room and that meant come morning the kids could wander in to flip on the TV.

"I can't go to sleep too early—what's your name?"

"Call me Lorrie. You won't bother her getting into bed after she's asleep. Autumn can usually sleep through anything. But she does wake up early."

"I can sleep through anything, too, so she won't bother me in the morning. I work late nights, you know, so I'm used to sleeping in."

Lorrie nodded. "Why don't you come up with me while I tuck her in. That way you'll know your way around. The bathroom's in the hall. I'll warn the boys to keep it picked up."

"I have a couple of suitcases," Cedra mentioned.

"Let me call Thad." Lorrie put Autumn to bed and showed Cedra the towel cupboard in the bathroom.

Cedra slid a pint of Wild Turkey from her suitcase. "Join me?"

Lorrie couldn't remember the last time she'd had a drink.

"Don't you corn-fed girls let your hair down once in a while?" she asked with a challenging grin.

Lorrie didn't think she'd sleep anytime soon herself. Perhaps a drink and a little conversation were just what she needed. She didn't want Cedra to think she was an unsophisticated country bumpkin. "Maybe one," she agreed.

She mixed her drink liberally with water and ice and the two of them sat on the lower deck near the pool.

Cedra lit a cigarette and the smoke wafted away in the darkening sky. "Orchards, huh? All those trees I saw driving in belong to you guys?"

Lorrie nodded.

"They're so small. Not at all what I'd have pictured. You know, you always think of people climbing ladders to pick apples."

"Many of them are dwarf hybrids. Others are pruned to stay close to the ground like that."

"The branches full of apples hang to the ground," Cedra said.

"Um-hm. Makes for easy picking. We need step stools only for the very top branches."

"Must take a lot of work to get them all picked."

Lorrie agreed. "We've all been out there with canvas bags. Your—" she wasn't sure what to call him "—Buzz and his dad have been sorting."

Cedra drew on her cigarette until the end glowed orange in the dark. "So this is what the good life that the Nebraska billboards advertise is all about."

The breeze lifted Lorrie's hair from her forehead. "I don't know how much of an example we are. Most of the population is in the cities. I have a sister in Omaha, and her life is nothing like mine. She's an actuary for a huge insurance company."

"Have a lot of family, do you?"

"Parents, sisters, everyone you met tonight."

Cedra slipped her sandals off and stretched her legs. "Well, your life here seems nice."

Lorrie sipped her drink. "I always thought so."

"I'll bet you were one of those girls who cheered the high-school football team on, fell in love with the tight end and had a June wedding with family and friends and—let's see, lavender-and-white flowers, and then you lived happily ever after."

"Almost," Lorrie said, uncomfortable that her life should look so cut-and-dried to this woman. "Dan—and Tom's mother'd had a stroke and wasn't doing well. We had a quiet wedding performed by a justice."

"In June?"

"First of August."

"Oh. A honeymoon?"

"Just a short one. But we did take a cruise on our tenth anniversary. He surprised me with flowers and the tickets."

"Sounds nice."

"It was."

"I mean him."

Lorrie glanced over. "Yeah. He is."

"Sorry about kissing him earlier."

Lorrie couldn't help the smile that came to her lips, remembering the look of surprise and then guilt on Dan's face. "No hard feelings."

"Good."

"As long as it doesn't happen again," Lorrie added, "now that you know the difference."

Not taking offense, Cedra smiled. She offered her glass and Lorrie clinked hers against it. "I would have figured it out, you know."

"What do you mean?"

"That he wasn't Buzz. I'd have known he didn't kiss the same."

"Would you?"

"Sure. Guys are all different, aren't they?"

Lorrie shrugged, a niggle of self-deprecating doubt creeping through her. Why hadn't she ever noticed that different kisses meant different brothers?

"I guess a marriage that couldn't handle a little thing like that wouldn't be much of a marriage, would it?" Cedra asked. "You seem like a confident person."

Lorrie traced a rivulet of condensation down the side of her glass and took a sip. "I don't know. I have my share of insecurities."

Cedra gave a dismissive little wave. "Oh, show me someone without an insecurity and I'll show you a psychopath."

Laughing out loud, Lorrie discovered that she liked this woman and her straightforward conversation. She didn't object when Cedra poured her another drink. "Tell me how you met—Buzz."

"Well, the guy he works for rented a party room at Rocking Em's for a Christmas get-together. The waitress called in sick that night, so I worked the room. After their party, Buzz hung around at the bar for a while, asked me to go have a sandwich after the place closed, and we did."

"So you liked him right off?"

"Oh, yeah. It was Christmastime, you know, and people without families, well, they either hang out together or end up alone. Buzz told me he never saw his family, and he didn't talk about you." In contrast to her dark hair, her skin appeared pale in the moonlight.

"He wouldn't have known I was family," Lorrie said. "I didn't marry his brother until after he was gone."

"But he never contacted his dad or Tom in all those years. Weird, huh?"

"I guess he didn't want any part of the orchards, and he made darned good and sure he got away."

"I still think it's weird. Why couldn't he just have said he didn't want to work here, and still kept in touch with his family?"

Lorrie shook her head. "I don't know. Gil was a lot more demanding back then. So was my father. Maybe the times have changed, or something."

"Thank goodness," Cedra responded.

"So you've been together since then?" Lorrie asked.

The other woman nodded. "He hasn't always been easy to live with. Gets a little moody now and then. We fight. We make up. Sex is great."

Lorrie's skin grew warm.

A choked little sound escaped Cedra and Lorrie quickly glanced at her. "Dammit, it hurts that he doesn't remember any of this!"

Without hesitation, Lorrie reached over and placed her hand on Cedra's arm. "He will, hon. He'll remember you. I know it."

Cedra released an embarrassed laugh and swiped at her eyes. "Yeah." She patted the back of Lorrie's hand. "Thanks."

They spoke for another half hour or so, until Lorrie couldn't control her yawns and excused herself. She made her way upstairs, washed and undressed and slid into bed.

Dan was hovering on the outer rim of sleep when Lorraine slid behind him, her silky skin warm and... bare. She fitted her knees into the curve of his bent legs, and her breasts flattened against his back. Between his shoulder blades he felt her breath and the touch of her lips.

She hooked her arm over his and brushed her palm across his chest. "Are you awake?" she asked.

"I am now."

Her fingertips brushed back and forth across his nipples. Dan's body responded immediately. God, he loved it when she touched him. These past days and nights had been a living nightmare. He'd been dreading her distaste for him, fearing her rejection and knowing he couldn't live without her love.

He raised his hips and assisted her in slipping his briefs off. She closed her fist around his ready shaft and he clenched his teeth in pleasure.

When he couldn't wait any longer, he turned and took her in his arms. She tipped her face up and he touched his lips to hers. "You've been drinking," he said with surprise.

"A little."

He could count on one hand the number of times he'd seen her tipsy. Neither of them drank more than an occasional cocktail or after-dinner drink. "Are you sure about this?"

"About what?"

He pressed himself into her belly. "About this."

"Don't you want me?"

"Lorraine." He kissed her and tasted bourbon. "I want you more than anything."

She raked her nails across his chest and down his abdomen. "What's there not to be sure of? It's not like we haven't done this before. Is there something about this part of our life you haven't told me?"

"No. I mean are you sure about how you feel about me? About this?" he said.

"No. I don't want to think about that now. I just want to feel good. And this makes me feel good."

"You make it sound like it's just good sex."

She flicked her tongue across his nipple, kissed a path to his chin and wedged her knee between his thighs. "It is good sex."

Dan caught her chin in his hand. "But it's more," he said. "It's love."

"Kiss me," she whispered.

He'd never had the willpower to deny her anything. He kissed her gently, but she wouldn't allow gentleness. She knew all the ways to make him crazy and urgent and mindless. He wanted her to admit she loved him, but she used his weakness to give him another, more demanding direction.

He gave himself over to her pleasure, because her pleasure was his. With long slow strokes, he drew her to the edge and waited for those tiny little noises in her throat and the allover tautening of her limbs.

He pulled away completely and teased her hardened nipples with his tongue. She held his head and pressed herself against him, trembling, her breath in scattered gasps. She was so beautiful in her excitement, so lost to the wonder of what they shared.

Her scent, her movements, everything about her set him on fire. He ran his hands over her, appreciating the soft womanly curves, the weight of her breasts, the turn of her hip beneath his palm. She had a woman's body now, not a girl's. She'd given him pleasure and children and love.

She reached for him and urged him back inside her, into the rhythm that took his breath and sent her over the edge with a wordless cry and an allover shudder.

Joining her, Dan waited for Lorraine to say his name, waited for the acknowledgement his heart craved more than this release his body needed. But she didn't say it.

She didn't say anything.

He allowed himself the lazy, spent sensation of lying atop her for only a minute before moving to her side. Brushing her hair from her temples with his fingers, he kissed her shoulder.

She shifted to her side, presenting her smooth bottom for him to curl himself around and cuddle as he had hundreds of times in the past. Dan almost wept at the sweet passion and familiarity of his love for her. But he kept it to himself this time.

In seconds she slept.

And in the morning she was gone.

* * *

"You know...I really feel like a Buzz. Buzz seems natural to me."

Lorrie's tawny eyes revealed no surprise. "You know, I think I'd feel comfortable calling you Buzz. I wonder how your dad would handle it."

He followed Lorrie across the lawn and watched her set the sprinkler and run back before it got her wet.

"I get the feeling that there was a lot of tension before I left. But now, I'm not sure. I wish I could remember, but it seems like the old guy's just glad to have me here."

"He is," she agreed.

"Lorrie, you got anything I can stick under this cast to scratch? I'm gonna lose my mind in about five seconds."

"Come on." She motioned him into the house. "We'll figure something out." She rummaged in a drawer and came up with a wooden stick.

"What is it?" he asked.

"A shish-kebab skewer."

He scratched his wrist and as far up his forearm as he could reach. "Oh, yeah..."

Lorrie grinned.

"Is she sleeping?" he asked.

Lorrie glanced up at him. "Cedra?"

He nodded.

"Yes. I got the impression she'd sleep most of the morning."

"Good. Not that I don't like her or anything," he hurried to say. "I just need a little time to think."

She gestured at the datebook and papers scattered across the table. "Well, take all the time you need. I have a lot of work to do, contacting the vendors for the Festival and giving them their booth assignments.''

''I wish I had this damned cast off so I'd be more help picking,'' he complained.

''I'm not helping with this last section either. Your brother said his crew could handle it this week. You can go down and help the boys. They're cleaning out the buildings.''

''I'll do that.''

''Shouldn't you be getting that cast off pretty soon?''

''Next week.'' He held up the skewer. ''Can I keep this?''

She curled her upper lip. ''Like I'd use it to cook with now. See you at lunch, *Buzz*.''

He grinned and headed for the huge barns. Out of everyone at Beckett Orchards, he felt most comfortable with Lorrie. He didn't know why. Every member of the family treated him well. She just didn't seem quite as nervous around him as his brother, and not as silent as his father.

It was bizarre having a brother who looked just like himself. Sometimes looking at Tom seemed so familiar, a sense of déjà vu would grip him. And then he'd think, well, of course Tom looked familiar: He was a mirror image of himself.

The snippets of vague recollections only made him more confused and frustrated. Like, why had he wanted a slice of that lemon chiffon cake so badly, when his father assured him that chocolate was his favorite? Thank goodness Lorrie let him be himself, whoever he was.

This Cedra gal wasn't unappealing. She had a sexy mouth and a body that invited exploration, and apparently he'd made the venture a time or two. He felt incredibly lonely. So out of sync with the rest of the world. Everyone else knew things about him he didn't. They all had personal knowledge of him—private things he didn't know himself—and that got him angry.

Maybe if they'd shut up for a while, quit trying to force things into his head that weren't there. Nobody wanted him to know all of it any more than he did himself.

But they meant well. And it was plain that they cared about him. It was just so damned hard to feel anything back, when they were all strangers.

He was at ease around the kids, too, so he enjoyed the day helping them sweep and hose out the buildings. None of them had been born before he'd left this place, so he was new to them as well as to himself, and they were getting to know each other in a more ordinary way.

Cedra showed up after lunch. "Want to take a drive with me, Buzz? I'm nearly out of smokes."

What the hell? "Sure."

She drove her Ford like she did everything, without a whole lot of preparation or thought.

"Would you mind slowing down a bit?" he asked. "I already have one broken arm."

She let up on the gas pedal. "You never used to mind my driving."

"Well, I mind it now."

She shrugged. "No problem."

In town, she stopped at a convenience store. "Want anything? A Coke maybe?"

"Sounds good."

She returned with two Cokes and a bag, from which she pulled a pack of cigarettes and opened them. She offered him the first one she loosened.

He shook his head.

A funny look crossed her face, but she stuck the cigarette between her shapely red lips and lit it, then started the engine.

"I suppose I used to smoke?" he asked.

"Yeah." She maneuvered the Taurus back to the highway. "Ever seen this Arbor Day place?"

"Not that I remember."

"It's supposed to be a historic landmark. Wanna check it out?"

He glanced over. Her black hair blew all spikey in the wind. She had an uncertain look on her face that she hid when she noticed him looking at her. "Yeah. Let's stop."

She smiled, a quick, contagious smile of genuine pleasure that lightened his mood.

Arbor Day Farm grew a miraculous assortment of trees, each labeled with species and origin. They walked the grounds and visited the fuelwood plant that operated the entire conference center. The Lied Center itself was a lovely, environmentally friendly hotel with a spectacular view of the surrounding countryside, including the Arbor Lodge.

The interior lobby had been constructed of breathtakingly enormous timbers, and even the carpets and door handles were of a leaf motif. They wandered in and out of a gift shop and paused in front of a restaurant.

"Have you eaten?" he asked.

She shook her head.

"Hungry?"

"I guess I am."

"Let's call and say we won't be back for supper," he suggested, then thought a second. "Do you have the number?"

"In my bag in the car."

"Let's get it."

He stood in the parking lot, watching her fumble through papers and datebooks and makeup. An envelope of photographs tumbled onto the back seat and he caught a glimpse of himself. "Is that me?"

She scooped up the pictures, almost embarrassed.

"Come on. Let me see." He opened his palm.

Cedra handed him the envelope.

He studied the color photographs carefully, one at a time. Himself watching an older woman blow out candles on a birthday cake. "Who's this?"

"Em. She owns the place I work at. That was her birthday."

Another showed himself, Cedra, and several others dressed in shorts and tank tops, holding a trophy and smiling at the camera.

"Our volleyball team," she explained.

He studied several more, ending with one of Cedra, dressed in tight jeans and a black leather jacket too large for her, in a sexy pose on a black SXS lowrider. He recognized it right off as the Harley his brother had hauled home in the back of his pickup.

For an instant, he could hear the rumble of the machine and feel the vibrations of the powerful engine.

"The police found some receipts with my things," he said. "I was in Trousdale for parts. I wonder if they were for my bike or one I was working on."

Cedra shrugged. "It was a Saturday. I was still asleep when you left. The guys at the shop said you hadn't mentioned where you were going. You'd told 'em you'd be in for a while in the afternoon, then you never showed up. I finally called the shop when it got late and they hadn't seen you. I didn't know what to think."

Her expressive brown eyes revealed things he thought she'd rather not have him see. Like insecurity. Love. She didn't know if he'd ever remember her or care for her again—if he ever had. How had he felt about her?

"The girls at Em's said you'd show up after a Saturday-night bender. I couldn't imagine anything like that. You'd never done it before. But I waited. And when you didn't come home on Sunday or go to work the next day, I got really scared and called the police. They weren't too concerned."

It was so strange to look at this proof of a life he couldn't recall. There could be no question that he'd been these places and done these things and known this woman. He was amazed at the things he knew and the things he didn't know. He knew every piece that made up a motorcycle. He could probably order them by part number without looking at a catalog. But he couldn't remember one specific bike.

Or sex. He had all the images in his head. He knew the textures and scents of a female body, what went where and exactly how great it felt. But he couldn't remember having sex with a particular woman.

Like this one...

His glance swept over her luminous eyes, her agreeable, luscious mouth and the shadow of cleavage at the front of her summer top. Of all the things to forget.

He took the envelope from her hand, stuffed the pictures back in, and tossed it on the back seat. "Let's go eat."

After Tom's call, Lorrie had driven into town and brought back burgers. The kids were thrilled with her supper choice. Tired from their day's work, they'd been waiting for the television premiere of a movie that was on that evening, and didn't want dish duty.

Gil had his own TV and settled himself in for the night.

"I have a lot of paperwork," Dan had told her, excusing himself after their late meal.

Lorrie completed several calls, reaching people she hadn't been able to get during the day. It grew late and she tucked Autumn and the twins in and left Thad reading in his bed. Instead of going into her room, she went back downstairs and noticed the fresh pot of coffee Dan must have brewed.

She poured two mugs and carried them into Dan's office.

He looked up. "Hi."

She'd avoided him since last night, embarrassed by her weakness at wanting him. She placed a mug on the corner of his desk and held the other. "Hi."

He laid his pen down and leaned back in his creaky office chair. "Thanks."

"Get a lot picked today?"

"Yep. Those college kids are great workers. I've already asked them to come back next summer."

"What are you working on?" she asked.

"Quarterly taxes."

"Oh." Lorrie knew other couples who operated farms. In many cases, the wife did the bookkeeping. She'd offered several times in the beginning, but Dan had insisted her time was best spent with the house and the children. Over the years it had become routine. Dan kept the books, did the taxes. She'd had so many things on her mind the past week, she hadn't thought to wonder about the complexities of Dan's deceit.

The legal ramifications struck her like a softball in the chest. She stared at him for several long minutes, gathering her apprehensive thoughts. "Are you going to be in trouble?" she asked finally.

"What do you mean?"

"With the IRS. What have you done? How could you have pretended to be Tom all these years and—"

"Lorraine."

She sat her coffee down. "What?"

"I'm not in any trouble with the federal government. Beckett Orchards is a corporation. I'm an employee, just like you and Dad and our pickers. I get a W-2 in my own name, all nice and legal."

"But how?" she asked, incredulous.

"I pay quarterly, so I keep a close eye on the figures. I can usually work the withholding so I break even, no money due me, none due them. If occasionally I have to pay, I get a cashier's check."

"What about our personal income tax?"

"I figure it and you sign it before me."

She thought about his reply. "I never realized. So you've used your own social security number?"

"Yes. It's all legal."

The knowledge was a great relief. But there were other considerations becoming apparent. "What about your driver's license?"

"It's in Tom's name. I'm actually using Tom's."

She nodded. "What about our marriage?"

She knew he'd dreaded the question. He forced himself to look her in the eye. "When we got our marriage license I used the new driver's license for identification. That's all I needed."

"You married me as Tom. Our marriage certificate says Thomas Beckett."

"That's right."

She waited for something more.

"We're not legally married."

Her supper sat like a rock in the pit of her stomach, and nausea rolled from her belly to her head. She found a place to sit beside a stack of sports magazines on the old sofa. "What about..." She looked up. "We've been living together for years. Aren't we married by common law?"

Dan shook his head. "There's no common-law marriage in Nebraska."

"What could happen to you?" she asked.

"There's no punishment, no jail time or anything. We're simply not married."

"You've checked into this, obviously."

He nodded.

Lorrie's neck ached with tension. She stood. "I'm really mad at you over this one!"

"A lot of people live together, Lorraine."

"We have children!"

"A lot of people have children without being married. It's not illegal."

She stiffened. "Well, I'm not a lot of people. How can you gloss this over like it's not important?"

"I didn't mean to do that. I'm sorry. I can only say I'm sorry in so many ways and with so much feeling. I am sorry."

Absently, she looked at the bank calendar on the wall, the framed photographs of their children on his cluttered desk, the engraved brass apple she'd given him for their anniversary. *Anniversary.* Anniversary of what? "So." She tilted her head away and then looked back at him. "You're not my husband."

The look that crossed his features told her she'd voiced something he'd hoped never to hear. He made no reply.

She didn't want to hurt him. She really didn't. Hurting him wouldn't fix any of this. It wouldn't make her feel better and it wouldn't change anything. She hurt as fresh and as bad as she had from the first minute she'd known. Hurting him wouldn't make her pain go away.

But if they were being honest, then let the chips fall where they may. Lorrie twisted her wedding rings from her finger. An empty glass dish which usually held pieces of hard candy sat on the desk. She calmly dropped the rings in. The sound of metal against glass rang in the silent room.

The muscles in Dan's jaw clenched visibly. He set his mouth in a white line. He was too much of a gentleman to mention that she'd climbed all over him in bed the night before, but it was on her mind . . . in her heart. . . .

She needed him. But she needed security. He loved her, but he'd shaken her foundation to the very core. Lorrie didn't know what was going to happen. Somehow her mind didn't move past this minute, past the hurt, no matter how much she willed it to. Her own helplessness angered her.

"Why did you do that?" he asked.

"They're just a symbol."

"Yes. Of what we've had all this time. That hasn't changed."

"They're a symbol of something that never was," she disagreed.

"Fine," he said, pushing his chair back. "Have it any way you want." It took him half a dozen good twists and finally a drop of oil from his top desk drawer before his gold band unscrewed from his finger. He took

Lorrie's hand and placed the warm metal in her palm. "There. We're not married. Feel better?"

The gold ring didn't have a lot of shine left. It was scratched and scarred like their relationship. She stared at it with her vision blurring. "No," she whispered, and left the room.

Chapter 8

There weren't enough words to fully describe Dan's feelings. Regret didn't begin to cover them. And sometimes, when he lay awake at night or when he paused over his work, he would wonder, if he had to do it all over again, how he would handle it. Would he do it differently? Tell Lorraine and Gil the truth and try to win her? Or would he take the years he'd had with her, regardless of the outcome?

Resignation came to mind most often when he tried to sort through his exhausting emotions. He'd dealt with nearly everything he could. There was still the question of telling Tom. Other than that, there was little he could do to fix what he'd done.

That Lorraine didn't think of him as her husband weighed heavily on his heart and affected his every waking moment.

The following week, Dan used a morning to clean the huge vats in the glass-walled pressing room with the pressure hose.

After lunch Thad and Tom joined him in inspecting the motors that ran the conveyor belts in the sorting room. He had taken one motor apart and had grease streaked to his elbows.

"Was the armature burnt?" Thad asked.

Dan grunted a negative reply.

"See if that wire's getting juice," Tom suggested.

Dan gave them both a look to quell their suggestions.

"I could have had that thing apart and back together an hour ago," Tom said.

"Yeah, well, now that your lily-white hand's out of that sling, help yourself," Dan countered.

"Don't want to get my nails dirty." The good-natured ribbing had been going on all afternoon. "Cedra makes me glad I have two hands again," Tom joked.

Thad laughed and Dan glanced up at his son, then his brother. "Watch it, those are adolescent ears listening."

"Aw, Dad." Thad and Tom watched Dan. "Did you two used to talk guy stuff when you were boys? You know, talk about girls and all that?"

"Sure we did," Dan said.

"Like what? What did you talk about?"

"Oh, about who we thought was hot, that kind of thing."

"You?" Thad laughed. "You talked about hot babes, Dad?"

"What's so funny about that?"

"Beverly Paulson," Tom said out of nowhere.

Dan stared at him. "What?"

"Beverly Paulson," he repeated. "She had a set of hooters that—"

"You remember her?" Dan asked incredulously. "What else? What else do you remember?"

Tom shook his head. "That's all." He looked thoughtful for a minute. "I just got this picture of her and her name was right there. I don't even know where I know her from."

"Eighth grade," Dan supplied.

Tom shrugged.

"That's it?"

His brother nodded. "That's it."

"You can't remember any of your family or where you went to school or anything about anything, but you remember Beverly Paulson's hooters?"

One side of Tom's mouth inched up. "They must have been some pretty remarkable hooters, eh?"

Thad laughed. "A blast from the past. Eh, Uncle Buzz?"

Tom hooked him around the neck with one arm and rubbed the knuckles of the other hand across the top of Thad's head. "Where'd you get this kid?"

"His mom found him under a cabbage leaf one day and begged me to let her keep him," Dan stated with a straight face. "So I did."

Tom released his nephew. "Do you believe that?"

Thad shook his head. "Uh-uh. I've seen the pictures. Gross!"

Dan shook his head. "Hand me those pins that hold the electrical brushes."

Thad obeyed. "Dad, how come you're not wearing your ring?" he asked.

Dan's hand paused only briefly. "It needed polishing. It's pretty nicked up."

A lie. He'd told his son a lie. What else could he have answered that wouldn't have frightened him?

Thad seemed to accept the explanation and went on to his next subject. "I've been wanting to ask you something personal."

Dan looked up. "We already had that talk about where babies really come from."

"Not that."

"Okay. Shoot."

"Well, some of the guys were talking about girls, you know..."

"Yeah?"

"And Jason Westfield said about this one girl that she stuffs it."

"You mean she puts something in her bra to make her look bigger."

"That's what it means, Dad." He rolled his eyes.

"Okay."

"Well, how can you tell? I mean, can you tell by looking?"

Tom snickered. "That's easy, Thad, you just get real close. Pretend you want to see something she's holding and brush the back of your hand or your arm across her."

Dan frowned at his brother. A couple of weeks ago he would have been worried that Thad was turning out just like Tom. But today he realized his son had the same healthy curiosity as any other boy his age.

"Well?" Tom grinned.

"That's not a good suggestion, Thad," Dan said. "You don't touch a woman unless she invites you to. It's a matter of respect."

"Well, then how can a guy know?" Thad asked. "I don't think this girl's going to invite me any time soon."

"I should hope not." Dan fitted the motor into its housing beneath a conveyor belt and motioned for the nuts and bolts. "Whether a girl has a little or a lot is really unimportant. When you fall in love with someone it doesn't matter. Besides, at thirteen, even if this girl does *stuff it,* she's still growing."

"Yeah." Thad fingered a bolt thoughtfully.

"I wonder if Cedra stuffed when she was thirteen," Tom speculated.

Dan couldn't help but join Thad in laughter. A part of Tom still existed, the part Dan loved and understood. Several times during the afternoon, it seemed as though nothing had changed, like goals and favoritism and years hadn't come between them.

Dan reached for the socket wrench. Tom was already holding it out to him, the half-inch socket he needed in place. Could have been his ace mechanic brain one step ahead of Dan. But more likely than that, it was that "knowing" thing they'd shared ever since Dan could remember.

They weren't mind readers, nothing as definite as that. It was more intuition than anything else. They picked up on each other's emotions. They answered a question before it was asked. Time and again, Dan would be thinking about something and Tom would bring it up. Not weird or anything. That's just the way it was between them.

And if that was still true, had Tom picked up on Dan's turbulent feelings recently?

Tom had been remembering a little here, a little there, for some time. So far nothing important. But he would. How much damage would it do for Dan to tell him the truth now? He didn't think it would make him remember. Nothing seemed to make him remember. Dan only considered telling him so that he'd be prepared when he did remember.

And he would.

Later, Dan scrubbed his hands at the metal sink in the tractor barn. He paused with the brush hovering over the back of his left hand and stared at the white band of skin on his ring finger. What did he care if Tom knew? How much more did he have to lose?

He finished washing.

"Mom's gonna take me to ball practice!" Thad hollered from the front of the building. "She said there's food in the oven."

Dan acknowledged him with a salute. He stepped out of the barn in time to see the Explorer heading down the drive. He trudged toward the house. If Lorraine hadn't taken Autumn, he'd need to keep an eye on her.

For most of the week, each step he'd taken, each thought he'd had, each chore he'd accomplished had meant nothing. If he wasn't Lorraine's husband, who was he? Somewhere in all of this mess he'd lost himself.

He was still Thad's father. He'd done a pretty fair job of parenting that afternoon. He was still Bram and Jori and Autumn's father, too. That was something he could take pride in.

He entered the kitchen to find the twins chasing each other around the table and Autumn fingerpainting the oak tabletop with melted red Jell-O.

"Did you eat yet?" he asked.

"Yep," Bram answered.

"Are the dishes done?"

"Nope," Jori replied. "It's his turn."

"Is not, it's yours. I did 'em last night."

He was still a father. "Mom did 'em last night. Do them together," Dan said, filling a plate from the dishes left in the oven. He sat beside his daughter. "Hi, munchkin."

"Hi, Daddy. Wanna play *Lion King* with me?"

"Is that a swimming pool game, too?"

"No, silly, it's a video game."

"Oh, okay."

He was a good father.

Did he have a hope of being a husband?

The next night they all went to Thad's ball practice and stopped for pizza afterward. Dan ordered and paid and Lorrie and Thad pulled tables together and arranged the chairs. "Where's our drinks?" Bram asked.

"Cedra's helping Dad," Lorrie replied.

"Oh, man, she's not strong enough to carry all those pitchers of pop!" Jori cried.

Everyone turned to look.

Cedra, in her short skirt and strappy sandals, gracefully wound her way through the tables with a tray of pitchers and glasses on one hand raised over her shoulder. Dan trailed behind with a tray of salad plates and silverware.

"She won't drop it," Tom assured him. "She can carry a tray of full pitchers in one hand, half a dozen beer mugs in the other, and dodge a bar fight at the same time."

Dan and Cedra reached the table in time to overhear Tom's comment. Cedra's eyes widened and she sat the tray down.

Dan and Lorraine looked at one another.

The kids, not noticing anything, took their glasses and plates.

Tom's eyebrows shot up as if he'd just realized what he'd said. "I *knew* that."

Cedra plopped into the chair beside him and laid a big kiss on his cheek. "Oh, sweetie, you're getting better!"

Dan sat across from Lorrie. She distributed the plates before looking at him. He wore a denim shirt with the sleeves cut off. He'd left his hat in the truck, but his dark hair still bore a ridge from it. She glanced at his hands, toying with a fork. Seeing the white ring on his finger filled her with a cold aching emptiness.

"Can Thad help me with my salad?" Autumn asked.

"Will you?" Lorrie asked her eldest son.

He agreed and they followed the others to the salad bar, leaving Dan and Lorrie alone for a moment.

"Shall I tell Tom?" Dan asked.

The thought gave Lorrie a panicky feeling in her chest. She didn't want to be the one to make the choice. Sometimes she thought he should know. Most times she feared the results. The effect on the children terrified her. If her world had been knocked off kilter by the news, what would it do to theirs?

"I don't think I'm ready," she answered truthfully. "But do what you have to."

He reached across the vinyl tablecloth and placed his hand over hers. To think that after all they'd shared, after all they'd done and been to each other, that that simple touch could make her heart skip a crazy beat amazed her. Lorrie refused to look at their hands.

"I don't think I'm ready yet, either."

His words eased her apprehension.

"Let's go get our food," he suggested.

"The Festival starts next week," Dan said while they were eating. "We'd better enjoy this time together."

The boys agreed around mouthfuls of pizza.

"I'm glad you're going to let me help." Cedra gave a little wave with her fork. "I know having an extra person around isn't easy. You've all been so nice to me and I appreciate it because I needed to be with Buzz. Working with you will make me feel like I'm doing my part."

"You haven't been any trouble," Lorrie said and meant it. Cedra had run Thad to ball practice a couple of times and she'd started helping with meals and dishes and laundry. She'd even picked apples and learned to sort.

"What will I do?" she asked.

"We'll show you and Buzz how to run the cash register out in the main room," Dan said.

"And the coolers constantly need refilling with gallon jugs of cider," Lorrie added. "You can watch the bagged apples and call for more of a variety when one runs out."

"Heck, I can handle that stuff." Cedra looked from one family member to another with an infectious grin.

Dan gave the kids quarters to play the video games.

"You didn't eat much again," Lorrie said to her father-in-law.

He shook his head. "Wasn't hungry."

Cedra chattered about someone back in Clarksville who could eat an entire large pizza without stopping for air.

Gil's plastic glass and remaining drink and ice hit the corner of the table and fell to the floor with a clatter.

Lorrie and Dan were beside him in an instant.

"Gil?"

"Dad, are you all right?"

"I don't know." He didn't sound all right. His face had turned a disturbing ashen color.

"I think we'd better get you to a doctor." Dan straightened.

"I agree." Lorrie looked around to see where the kids were.

"I'll take them home," Cedra offered.

Lorrie glanced at Gil's bloodless face and then at Dan.

"She can drive the Explorer home. We'll take her car." He dug in his jeans pocket for the keys.

Lorrie accepted Cedra's key ring. She took a moment to tell Thad what was going on. "Keep the others calm and get them ready for bed," she said.

"I will. Don't worry," he told her.

It was such a grown-up thing for her son to say, it touched her. Proud of him, she smiled and gave him a hug. "We'll call if we're gone long."

She joined Dan in helping his father to the door and noticed Tom hung back. "Coming?" she asked.

"I don't know where I'd do the most good." A frown creased his brow.

"Do what you want to," Lorrie said.

"I'll come with you." He stepped ahead and held the glass door open.

They situated Gil in the front passenger seat of Cedra's car, fastened his safety belt and reclined the seat. Lorrie handed Dan the keys and climbed into the cluttered back seat with Tom. The ride seemed to take forever, even though, gratefully, they'd been right in town where St. Mary's hospital was only minutes away.

The emergency-room nurses didn't seem overly concerned when Lorrie ran in and asked for assistance. A middle-aged nurse located a wheelchair and walked ahead of Lorrie, her white shoes squeaking.

She wheeled Gil inside and down a hall. The attendant at the window told them to have a seat and fill out admittance papers.

"Not exactly *E.R.*, is it?" Lorrie mumbled to Dan, her hand resting at the small of his back.

"You and Tom go on back with him," Dan suggested. "I'll do this."

She nodded and hurried away, knowing he knew more about insurance matters than she did.

By the time Dan finished answering all the questions, Lorraine returned and led him to a tiny waiting room where Tom sat. "They think he had a minor heart attack." She took his hand without thinking. "They gave him nitroglycerin to get his blood pressure down. They have to do tests to see if there's any damage to the heart muscles."

Dan squeezed her hand.

"You go in with him for a little while," she suggested.

Dan followed her directions and found his father lying on a gurney in a curtained-off antiseptic-smelling room. A long plastic oxygen tube ran from beneath his nose to a plate in the wall. Beside him, a young redheaded nurse took his blood pressure.

"Hey, Dad."

"Bad timing, I know," Gil said.

"What do you mean?"

"Festival's next week."

"Don't worry about that. I can handle everything."

Gil nodded. "I know you can, son."

Dan watched the nurse fasten sticky electrode pads to Gil's chest.

"I've heard about men who had the big one right in front of the doctors and there's no help for it," Gil said.

"Dad, that's not going to happen. You're right here under their supervision."

"We're not going to let anything happen to you, Mr. Beckett," the freckled nurse said.

Ignoring her, Gil met his son's eyes. "I have to say something."

"Okay."

"I'm not very good at this."

"You don't have to say anything. All you have to do is rest and let these people take care of you."

"Yeah, I do. I have to say this."

Dan shrugged and waited.

"I didn't give you credit, all those years ago. I thought . . . well, I thought you were too wrapped up in yourself and having a good time to give the orchards what they deserved."

Dan's heart pounded and he wondered if he'd be the next one with a nitroglycerin tablet shoved under his tongue. His father had never spoken to him like this, and considering the situation he'd created for himself, he'd been grateful.

"You did the right thing, after all," his father went on. "I worked my whole life, planting trees and waiting and planning for the place to really be something. If you hadn't taken over, I'd have had to sell years ago."

Dan didn't know what to say. He loved the land and the trees more than his father knew, more than he should have as Thomas Beckett.

"Sometimes I've felt so bad," Gil went on, "about pressuring you into this life. But you always looked like you were happy."

"I have been happy," Dan replied honestly. "There's nowhere I'd rather have been than here."

Gil looked a bit more relaxed. "I never understood why Dan just up and ran off the way he did. I acted mad, but it hurt me, him leavin'. Why do you think he left?"

"Why do you think he left?" Dan countered.

"I wondered if he had feelings for Lorrie, and he couldn't stand seeing the two of you together."

The idea was more perceptive than Dan would have given him credit for. Dan couldn't respond. The old man was lying in the emergency room being treated for a heart attack! This was hardly the time and place for Dan to point out that he'd been on the short end of the favoritism stick for nineteen years. How ironic that the son Gil now heaped praise on for holding the family business together hadn't made any kind of a sacrifice at all. He'd done exactly what he'd wanted to do, even at the expense of hurting Lorrie and their children.

Awareness of his father's mortality struck him with a vengeance. He would die eventually, whether now or later, and for the first time, Dan realized how much it would hurt him for Gil not to know it had been him all this time. He, not Tom, had worked the orchards and seen to it they became prosperous.

Dan tried to swallow the old jealousy that rose up. What was in a name, after all? His father was praising *him* for his hard work, not Tom.

And leave it to his father not to take any of the responsibility for his son's leaving. Of course, in his mind, it was less understandable that Dan would leave, rather than Tom.

"A lot of people asked me why he left," Dan admitted. "I told them I didn't know. Maybe he didn't even know. Maybe it was just one of those rash decisions we all make and he's had to live with it ever since."

"I love him," Gil said. "As much as I love you. I don't know why I expected more of you."

Dan lowered his head, frustration consuming him. In all the years he'd lived as Dan, he couldn't remember his father telling him he loved him. Why now? And why to the son he thought was Tom? He closed his eyes and tried to remember how many times he'd told his children he loved them.

"I worried about him all this time," Gil said.

Dan couldn't look up.

"I've worried if he was safe. If he was happy. If he'd given me any more grandchildren. I wondered if I'd see him again before I died."

"Well, you don't have to worry about him any more." Dan tried to get him off the confusing subject. "He's obviously done all right for himself. Pretty soon he'll get his memory back and everything will be fine."

"Maybe he'll remember why he didn't want to be here and leave again," Gil said.

"Maybe." Dan watched the nurse hook a small plastic bottle to the oxygen connection at the wall. "What's that for?"

"Moisture, so his nose and sinuses don't dry out."

"Oh." The water bubbled energetically when the oxygen hit it.

"I'd like for him to remember some of the good things we did together," Gil went on, not seeming to notice any of the procedures. "Before your Ma got bad."

"I'm sure he will." Dan didn't want to be reminded of his mother's decline and death right now, not while he waited for the report on his father's heart damage.

"I was hard on him," Gil said. "I was hard on you both, and I thought I was doing the right thing."

"None of that matters now, Dad. Please, just rest." He stood to leave.

"Send Lorrie back in."

"Okay."

"She's a good girl. I knew she was a good girl from the first time her daddy brought her to the Legion post. Funny how he got all girls and I got two boys, isn't it?"

Dan had never heard his father ramble on so.

"Only seemed right we should match 'em up." Gil raised a hand. "Have you ever been sorry...about marrying Lorrie?"

Dan turned back. "Not for a minute. Ever."

Gil slanted a weak smile. "Good."

The doctor assured them that the damage to Gil's heart was minimal, but they wanted to keep him for more tests, and to get his edema and blood pressure down.

They saw him situated in a post-intensive-care room, and Tom drove home. Lorrie sat in the back, among Cedra's bags and papers, and listened to the brothers' quiet conversation.

"I think we should give him my office downstairs," Dan said. "That way he wouldn't have to climb the steps."

"We should ask the doctor first," Tom said. "Maybe the exercise is good for him."

Dan shrugged. "We'll ask."

Cedra waited in the kitchen, the Letterman show blaring from the portable television on top of the refrigerator. Tom turned it down.

"The kids are all asleep," she said.

Lorrie started a pot of decaffeinated coffee. "Thanks."

Dan didn't say much while they sat at the table. He sipped from his mug and listened to the others.

"I'm going out to smoke." Cedra grabbed her purse from the counter.

"I'll go with you." Tom refilled his cup and followed.

Lorrie placed her and Dan's cups in the dishwasher. Dan flipped off all but the light over the stove, and climbed the stairs after her.

Lorrie came out of their bathroom to find him gone. She glanced out at the empty deck, then padded down the hall. It had grown far too late for him to go to his office to work.

In the darkness, his tall silhouette came from Bram and Jori's room. "What's wrong?"

"Nothing," he whispered, and led her back to their bedroom. He slid out of his boots and shirt.

"Are they awake?"

"No." He placed his watch on his dresser.

Lorrie folded the coverlet down and climbed into bed.

"I just wanted to look at all of them." He sat on the edge of the bed and turned toward her. "Do you think they know how much I love them?"

"Of course they do," she said with surprise.

"Do I tell them enough? Do I show them every day?"

The tenderness and all-consuming passion she harbored for this man had not changed. The emotions rose in her chest with a quick sting of tears behind her eyes. The events of the evening had pushed everything else aside. In her concern, she'd forgotten her own distress and anger. She and Dan had behaved like two people who cared for Gil. And for each other. After all the turmoil of recent days, their former relationship had come through.

"You're a wonderful father." She worked to keep her voice from trembling. "Each one of your children is secure in your love. You've spoiled Autumn rotten, treating her like a little princess. You show Bram and Jori equal attention and affection. Have you realized how non-competitive they are with each other? Their silly bantering is just normal behavior for kids."

He seemed to consider her words.

"And Thad," she said with a sigh. "Even though you believed he wasn't yours for all that time, you were patient and understanding. What more could a son want than a father who loves him and supports him, even if he chooses to do something other than what the father had hoped?"

"Is it obvious?" Dan asked quickly. "That I'd like to see him stay here?"

"It's only normal," she replied. "You want to see your land and trees stay in the family. But you care more that Thad is fulfilled in whatever he does."

Dan nodded.

Lorrie studied his fatigued expression. "Sometimes I think you feel more of Tom's feelings than he does himself."

He looked at her. "What do you mean?"

"The pressure you're so careful not to place on Thad is what your father did to Tom to drive him away."

"Yes."

"And you feel Tom's pain."

"I felt it then."

"More than your own?"

"No. That's why I'm careful to treat the twins equally. I don't want one of them to ever feel the way I did. Any of them, for that matter."

They were silent for a few minutes.

"Come to bed," she said. "It's late."

Dan slid off his jeans and doused the light. The bed shifted with his weight.

Lorrie blinked into the darkness overhead.

"He said he loves Dan," he said. "Said it hurt him when he left." She heard him swallow. "Why couldn't he have told me fifteen or twenty years ago that he loved me, Lorraine?"

"I don't know."

"I'm just blaming him for my stupid choices, aren't I?"

"Maybe."

"Like if I'd been more confident about who I was, I wouldn't have denied my own identity."

"Maybe you wouldn't have."

"But it's not his fault."

"Not entirely."

"Not at all."

"You don't have to feel guilty about being angry with your father," she said.

"I'm not mad at him," he denied.

"Well, you should be."

"Why?"

"Because he hurt you. Because he showed favoritism and you can't understand that. You don't know what was wrong with you that he didn't choose you as his favorite."

"I was the one who loved the orchards," he admitted.

"You were the one who stayed in school to please him."

"I was the one who took his orders and learned how to do things."

"You were also the one close enough to see what Tom's rebellion was doing to Gil, how much it hurt him."

Long minutes of ponderous silence passed.

"He told me what a good job I've done."

"You have."

"But he's really thanking Tom."

"No, he's really thanking *you*. *You're* the one who stayed and worked and made something of Beckett Orchards."

"He could die not knowing that," he said hoarsely.

"Do you want to tell him?"

"No. I don't want to tell him."

He seemed certain.

"I want him to know himself." His voice held a hurtful quality he'd never before revealed. "I want him to have known from the beginning that I'm Dan. I want him to have loved me enough and paid attention enough to know without me telling him."

Lorrie ached for Dan's unhappiness. She scooted closer and reached for him. Her fingers found his cheek wet with tears. "Oh," she said softly and pulled him against her.

He pressed his face to her chest and his shoulders shook with silent sobs. Lorrie didn't know what to do, what to say to comfort him. He was so big in her arms, so solid and male, and yet he seemed different this way, vulnerable and genuine. She kissed his hair and his temple and rubbed his bare shoulder soothingly.

Was this how he felt about her, too, wishing she'd known who he was without being told? Had her ignorance hurt him as much as his father's?

She held him, glad to be here for him, glad to have him turn to her with his doubts and disappointments.

Strangely, with everything that had come to light, they'd never been as close as at that moment. Nothing stood between them. No lies. No hidden secrets. They shared a family, a bed.

Dan's hand moved to cover her breast through her cotton nightshirt. Against her hip, she felt his body respond. He hooked his fingers behind her neck and inched himself upward to kiss her. Drawing comfort from each other came as the most natural thing in the world.

Lorrie met his passion with her own, as she always had. She knew the texture of his lips and skin better than her own. Their enthusiastic joining was familiar and reassuring. Only one thing was different from all the times before: she knew he was not her husband. By the time they laid entwined, breathless and satisfied, the tears were Lorrie's.

Chapter 9

"Need any caffeine, Buzz?" Cedra opened a Coke and sat beside him on the back porch.

He didn't mind the sultry evening air, and in fact, enjoyed the droning sound of the locusts in the groves. "No thanks."

"A snack? I could fix you something."

He shook his head.

"You all right?"

"Yeah."

"Upset about your old man?"

"More like confused, I guess," he said honestly. Gil's spell had affected the entire household. The old man was his father, and he knew he should be feeling something more than he was. "Upset that I probably should be more upset than I am."

"Nothing about these people or this place rings a bell with you? Your graduation picture is on the wall in the hallway."

"No." Looking at the old photographs had been nothing short of eerie. They made him think he recognized himself at that point of his life, but the recollection was so vague it disturbed him. "The first time I saw any of them was a few weeks ago."

"Funny you never mentioned any of them to me before—when you could remember, I mean. You told me you were from Nebraska and that you didn't keep in touch with your family. I thought they must be real jerks or something, but they're so nice."

"Cedra, please."

"What?"

"Stop pushing me."

"I'm not pushing you, I'm just wondering why you didn't tell me about them. Having an identical twin isn't exactly forgettable."

"Obviously, it is, because I've forgotten it, haven't I?"

"You know what I meant." She sipped her Coke. "I miss the way it was between us. I miss being with you. Sleeping with you." Her words hung between them until she spoke again. She picked at the label on the plastic bottle with her thumbnail. "Maybe if we—you know—you'd remember."

Sleeping with her at this point didn't seem fair to either one of them. Not that the thought was unpleasant by any means, it was just that he didn't want to have sex only for the sake of having sex. And an added dimension to their relationship could confuse him more than ever. "I don't think so."

"What could it hurt? We've done it plenty of times."

"Did you nag me like this before?"

She stood. "Go to hell."

"Where are you going?"

"Up to my room like a good little girl."

He caught her wrist. "Sorry. Sit down."

She complied.

He scooted the rattan chair he sat in until he could reach to place his feet on the banister. "It wouldn't be fair to you or to me, Cedra. I'm sorry if it hurts you that I don't remember. I just can't force anything. The doctors at the university said not to try to force my memory to come back. I do memory-skill exercises twice a week, and they're supposed to help. Anything more is just too frustrating."

Her pulse beat gently in his grasp and he turned her hand over and entwined their fingers. "It's not that I wouldn't like to. I think you're really sexy."

Reluctantly, she smiled.

"I really don't want to hurt your feelings, it's just that I don't want to complicate things any more than they already are."

"I'm sorry, Buzz."

"It's all right. I know this is hard for you, too." He lowered his feet to the porch floor and leaned over to kiss her.

She kissed him back with a surprising sweetness. She touched his cheek with cool fingertips and smiled half-heartedly. "Being friends is okay, Buzz. I can use a good friend."

He agreed, and kissed her fingers.

On Monday morning, Dan sat in the hospital waiting room, a cup of cold coffee on the magazine-cluttered glass table beside him. An irritating talk show squawked from the television hung from the ceiling. He'd never been a very patient waiter. Thank God he'd been in with Lorraine each time she'd given birth, because he'd have lost his mind waiting helplessly.

Lorraine appeared and sat in the chair beside him and he straightened. The fresh scent of jasmine drifted to him, a welcome change from the hospital smells he'd endured for hours. "Hi."

"Hi. Have you heard anything yet?"

He shook his head. "They didn't even bring him down from his room until about an hour ago. The doctor said the heart catheterization itself only takes about twenty minutes or so. I guess we're waiting on the emergency cases ahead of him."

"That's a good sign. At least he's not an emergency."

"True." He tapped his fingers on his thigh. "This test will tell us if he has any blockage anywhere in his heart."

A door opened and Dan looked up. A doctor in green scrubs came out and spoke with a family across the room. Dan turned his attention back to Lorraine. "I hate leaving you with all the work like this." He gave her an apologetic shrug. "I don't know what else to do."

"This is where you should be," she replied. "Try not to worry about it. We're handling everything. I got the floor chalked off for the booths, so the barn is ready for the renters to come in and set up."

"When did you tell them they could get in?"

"Tomorrow and Wednesday so they have time to decorate and put their stuff out. My mom and sisters have two booths for all their quilts and needlepoint crafts. Did you eat?"

He'd been gone before breakfast that morning. He shook his head. Lorraine opened her purse and handed him an apple. Dan looked at the Wealthy, his favorite to eat fresh, and her unfailing thoughtfulness touched him. He smiled. "You're getting more like your mom all the time."

"Scary, isn't it?"

He wanted to take her hand or wrap his arm around her or touch her face.

Instead he ate his apple.

Another hour passed before the doctor came out. He sat on a chair positioned at an angle to them. "We found some blockage in two of the arteries, so we did the angioplasty," he explained. "Your father signed permission for the procedure as a precaution."

Dan sat forward. "I thought you'd send him to Omaha for surgery."

"Angioplasty isn't surgery," the doctor replied. "It's done through the same shunt that we place in the groin for the catheterization. There's only one tiny incision."

"So it's over?" Dan asked.

"All over. He was awake throughout, and he'll just be a little groggy. In most cases, the ballooning works to open up fatty deposits in the arteries and get the blood flowing again. He'll have to lie still for eight hours, since we did go in through an artery, but he should be able to go home tomorrow."

Dan and Lorraine looked at each other in amazement.

"The dietitian will go over his eating with you, and your father will have to develop some better habits, but he'll do just fine."

Relieved, Dan stood, shook the physician's hand and thanked him. He sat back down beside Lorraine. "I guess maybe I overreacted," he said finally.

"What do you mean?"

"I mean last night."

"Not at all," she said softly. "You've never been ashamed of your feelings before. Don't get macho on me now."

He glanced at her and she grinned.

Before long, a nurse let them know Gil had been returned to his floor. Dan led Lorraine to the room. His nurse placed new sticky pads for the cardiac monitor on Gil's chest and took his vital signs. "Now, don't move your leg, Mr. Beckett," she warned. "I'll be back in a few minutes to check on you."

"Well, I made it." Gil flexed the bruised hand that held his IV.

"We knew you'd make it." Lorraine patted his foot through the thin white blanket. "You haven't worked all these years just to die and miss enjoying the fruit of your labors."

He chuckled at her pun.

Gil grew sleepy and Lorraine told him to rest. Someone would be back that evening to check on him.

"You can work the rest of the afternoon and this evening," Lorraine said to Dan as if she knew his thoughts as they crossed the lobby.

"It's a good thing we have Tom to help. Where'd you park?"

She pointed to the Explorer beneath a shade tree. "And Cedra."

"And Cedra. The Festival will seem strange without Dad helping." Gil had always been a part of Dan's life. They'd worked side by side since he could remember. This whole thing had been a major scare.

"Your dad may or may not be able to help at all anymore. But at least he's alive."

She'd worn her hair loose, and the breeze fluttered the silken tresses becomingly. Her eyes appeared as warm as rich honey in the sunlight. "Can I hold you?" Dan asked impulsively.

Her expression barely altered. She stepped into his embrace, her arms around his waist, her head against his chest.

Dan inhaled her fresh, familiar scent, cupped her head in his palm, and held her body close, drawing strength and comfort. She had always been there for him, was still there for him, even with the knowledge of what he'd done. "I love you, Lorraine," he whispered.

She remained in his arms, but she didn't speak. Finally, she drew back, and with her palms flattened on his chest, looked up at him. "I'm doing the best I can," she said softly. Finally, she pulled away. "Nothing feels solid anymore." Her gaze remained riveted to his. "If you're not who I thought you were, then I'm not who I thought I was, either."

Dan hurt more for her than he did for himself. How selfish he'd been, regretting only the effect this had had on him—how he missed her love and trust. At least he'd known the truth all along, and prepared himself for the possibility of discovery.

"Can you understand that?" she asked.

Lorraine hadn't known. She'd flourished in life, unsuspecting that one day stability would be ripped out from beneath her. She'd been totally unprepared for her world to turn upside down. That she even cared if he understood or not told him more than her words.

"I do understand," he answered. He understood perfectly. And that placed them at another stalemate. "Thanks for being here. Thanks for caring."

She whisked a long strand of hair away from her mouth. "Where else would I be?"

They were a family. In spite of Dan's masquerade, this was Lorraine's reality. *Her family.*

She pulled her keys from her purse, got in the Explorer, and backed it out of the space. Dan waved before finding his pickup.

Rolling down the windows, a sizable portion of his heavyheartedness dissipated in the sunny air. His father was going to be all right. And Lorraine still cared for him.

He placed his hat on his head and drove toward home with a smile touching his lips. Amazing what a little hope could do for a person's outlook.

Lorrie and Cedra brought Gil home from the hospital late Wednesday and set him up in the family room. Tom took Gil's bed for the time being. The Festival opened on Thursday, cars from surrounding counties filling the gravel parking area.

That night, Lorrie had food warming when the others finally came to the house. Cedra ate a small portion and excused herself to the porch.

"Is Dad sleeping?" Dan asked.

Lorrie nodded. "He conked out a little before ten."

"I didn't even get to talk to him today."

"We'll eat breakfast together in the morning," Lorrie promised. "Then, why don't you come up to the house for a lunch break?"

"That's a good idea. You can get by without me for half an hour or so."

"Did we do this when we were kids?" Tom asked.

Dan looked over. "Do what?"

"Work the Festival like your kids do."

"We only started the Festival about ten years ago," Dan replied. "Before that we had a barn we sold out of, like a truck garden. And yeah, you and I worked summers picking and sorting and selling apples.''

Tom looked thoughtful.

"You never much liked it," Dan told him.

"I didn't?"

"You always had somewhere else you'd rather be, something you'd rather do." Dan glanced at Lorrie and she wondered if he realized what a fine line he was treading by telling Tom his own history instead of Dan's. Apparently he did, because he grew silent. "I'm beat. I'm gonna shower and hit the sack."

"See you in the morning," Tom said.

Lorrie put the last of the dishes in the dishwasher. "'Night."

After her own shower, she flipped on the television and curled up in bed.

"How did Dad seem to you today?" Dan asked from beside her.

"A little bored. These weeks will be the hardest for him, because we're all so busy."

"I don't know what we can do about that. We can't spare anybody. Can we?"

"Well..." She thought a minute. "Why don't we all take our breaks up here? I could just leave the lunches in the fridge instead of hauling the cooler down."

"The walk will take too much time from our breaks," Dan said. "And the kids can't drive it. Come the weekend, we'd have to fight the traffic getting in and out."

They lay for several minutes, getting sleepy, not paying attention to the TV.

"I know!"

Lorrie turned to Dan. "What?"

"We'll take the mopeds down to the barns. That way, it'll be a quick ride up to the house."

They owned two lightweight motorbikes that the kids rode occasionally for fun. Lorrie had taken turns and knew how to handle one. "That's a great idea."

He flipped off the lamp, rolled over tiredly, and mumbled, "Yeah, well, consider the source."

"It must be exhausting being a genius." Lorrie smiled at the back of his head. "Good night."

A soft snore was his reply.

The first time he showed her how to do the bank deposit, they were sitting on stools behind the counter in the air-conditioned gift shop, the register readings in front of them, cash and checks counted and stuffed into a zippered pouch. Dan watched her tally the total on a small adding machine and write the figure in the blank provided on the deposit slip.

Taking the paper from her, he signed his name and handed it back. Lorrie stared at the signature. Finally, she looked up.

Her honey-gold gaze inspected his hair, his face, his mouth, poring over him as if she'd never really seen him before. At that moment, he wished he could read her eyes, understand what she was thinking, what she thought of him now. Now that it was real to her.

"When I look at Tom," she said, surprising him with the subject, "I wonder how in the world I could have missed it. He doesn't look like you—oh, I know he *looks* like you, that's not what I mean. I mean, he's not you, and it's so obvious to me now."

Dan didn't say anything. He took the paper from her fingers and tucked it into the bag with the money.

"If I'd known him better, I would have realized," she said. "We all saw one another at the pancake suppers and fish fries and fund-raisers while we were growing up, you know. And then high school. But Tom and I really only dated for a few months, and part of that time he was away at college. We went to the movies, we attended school functions. He was pretty...aloof, now that I look back on it. Of course, I understand now that Gil was pressuring him into seeing me. Right?"

Reluctantly, Dan nodded.

"My dad was doing the same thing to me," she admitted. "God, I've thought about this so much."

Dan recognized the insecurity and bewilderment she'd experienced initially. But her tone and her words lent him hope that she was coming to terms with the situation.

"That one time with him—"

"Don't, Lorraine—"

"I want to say this."

He didn't want to hear about his brother taking her virginity. He didn't want to face the fact that anyone but himself had had the privilege of intimacy with the woman he loved. But if she needed to say it, he would listen. They had no one but each other to confide in. He gave her his full attention.

"We'd been to a game in Lincoln, and afterwards one of those tailgate parties, you know, where everyone brings beer, and has a good time. I never drank much, so a couple of them went to my head, and I asked Tom to take me home.

"We stopped somewhere. It was dark and I wasn't quite sure where we were."

There were a dozen deserted places where couples had parked; Dan could only guess.

"I don't remember it all perfectly—it was so long ago. But I remember being convinced that if what our fathers wanted was for us to get together, that having sex with him was the right step. And, yes, I was infatuated with Tom. He was fun and popular and good-looking. And persistent.''

Dan studied his hands, palms pressed together.

''So I went along with it.'' She sat, thoughtful for a moment. ''I've looked back on it as both sordid and innocent.''

''What do you mean?'' he asked without looking up.

''Well, I—we didn't even have our clothes off. It was just sort of hurried and clumsy. But...''

He looked up. ''But what?''

''But I didn't know anything different. I thought, 'Is this what I've been saving myself for? Is this what all the locker-room talk and the big hoopla is about?' It was messy and uncomfortable and I really didn't care if I ever did it again.''

As detestable as Dan found the image, he was grateful to know what had really happened. ''But you felt something for him, Lorraine. You wouldn't have done it if you hadn't.''

''Yes. I felt something for him. Some naive hopeful thing. And I was scared the chance for marriage would pass me by. I was never sure he felt anything for me. That's why when he—I mean when you proposed to me, I couldn't believe it. I'd thought maybe you'd just call it off between us or—or I didn't know what.''

''And now?'' he asked, taking the biggest risk he'd ever taken. ''Do you feel anything for him now?''

She contemplated Dan's face for a long, hard, agonizing minute. ''Embarrassed. I'll die when he remembers me.'' She looked at her hand and back at him. ''Concern. He's your brother, after all.''

Dan waited for something more.

"I don't love him, if that's what you mean. Not like that, anyway. I love him like an in-law." She shook her head, wryly. "Even though he's not really, is he? Not legally."

"What about me?"

"What about you?"

"Do you love me?"

She looked away.

"Lorraine, don't punish me by withholding your love."

"I'm not punishing you."

"Then say it. If you love me, damn it, say it."

She kept her gaze on the counter. "I love you. All right, damn it! I love you."

She'd said it. The way she'd said it, the way he'd forced her to, struck Dan as humorous, and he couldn't help a chuckle. Maybe it was nervous relief, but cussing at each other was suddenly the funniest thing that had happened all week. He laughed out loud.

"You're losing it, Beckett." She stood and zipped the deposit bag, a smile on her own face.

He wanted to pull her against him and hug her tight. But it hadn't been that way between them for a while. They were lovers, in the dark secret cloak of night. But they were no longer friends.

"I'll run this to the depository."

"Take someone with you."

She looked back.

"Just to be on the safe side."

"Thad?"

"Thad'll do just fine."

She nodded and left the shop. Dan locked the cash drawer in a cabinet under the counter and turned out the lights. He still had a couple of hours of work before he finished for the night, but the prospect didn't seem like a burden.

He felt like his dad must have felt when they got all the fluid away from his heart. He was breathing easier tonight.

Lorraine still loved him.

Chapter 10

On a Wednesday three weeks later, Lorraine went to shop and see a movie in Omaha with her sisters. Dan cleaned the presses, stocked the coolers, and prepared for the final weekend. Even though the Festival operated Thursday through Sunday, the rest of the orchard's operation had to be handled on the other days.

Tom and Cedra had gone somewhere for dinner and Dan and Gil fixed a meal for themselves and the children. Lorraine's sister Lorna's five-year-old daughter had come for the night while her mother was gone, and the girls giggled over something Jori had said.

"You had a record crowd this year." Gil pushed his food around with his fork.

"Our net sales are already higher than last year, and we have another four days left." Dan eyed the baked potato on his father's plate. "Use the salt and butter substitutes and eat that."

"They can't really expect people to eat this crap," Gil complained. "What pleasures are left to an old man who can't eat what he likes?"

"It's not that bad." Dan shook the shaker over his own potato and tasted it. Couldn't hurt to develop better habits before he had a problem like his dad's. "I'm sure you must get used to it."

Gil grumbled, but he ate.

"Dad, the red moped keeps killing out." Thad forked another slice of tomato onto his plate. "Can you help me look at it?"

"I don't know when I'll have time, but we'll do it first chance I get," Dan promised.

Satisfied with that reply, his son finished his meal and excused himself. Bram and Jori followed him out the back door.

"Me and Jackie are gonna play Barbies now, awright?" Autumn asked, taking her cousin's hand.

Dan got out of his chair and knelt to give each a hug. "Just don't play beach in the bathroom this time, okay?"

"We won't," freckle-faced Jackie piped up. "We're gonna play baby-sitters."

He watched them skip off, only slightly reassured that their current pretend game would be less messy than the last, when they'd carried buckets of sand from Autumn's sandbox to the bathtub and created a swimming area for their dolls.

He and Gil cleared the table. Thad returned and the three of them played a couple of games of Yahtzee before it grew dark and the kids went up to sleep.

Dan stretched out on his stomach on the bed and watched his favorite home videos, backing the tapes up and rerunning several places. The twins' first birthday always made him laugh. Even then, Bram had been more laid back, hesitant and wide-eyed over the colorfully frosted cake on the table. A five-year-old Thad fed him a taste of frosting from the tip of a spoon and he grinned and waved his chubby arms.

Jori, on the other hand, caught sight of the cake and before anyone could stop him, grabbed two fistfuls and jammed them in his mouth. Watching, Dan laughed along with the voices on the tape, and laughed harder when Jori grabbed another handful of cake and plopped it directly on top of Bram's head.

Memories of happy times flashed across the screen: Thad learning to ride a bike; a much thinner Gil waving from the cab of their old Ford truck; Lorraine, flushed and glowing, holding newborn Autumn in her arms; their trip to Dallas; the kids on amusement park rides. So ordinary.

So special.

Dan slipped in another cassette. He'd watched this one so many times, he knew exactly what was going to happen, how the voices sounded, had memorized the colors and the expressions. After he'd taken the footage, he'd never been able to show it to anyone but Lorraine, and she'd blushed furiously.

After a few scenes of the boys playing softball in the yard came a shot of the bathroom door in the hallway. Behind the door, soft voices could be heard. The door opened and the camera jiggled a little as Dan wedged it into the opening.

Autumn and Lorraine sat in a tub full of bubbles, Lorraine's hair piled on her head, wet tendrils stuck to her neck. A thick lather enveloped Autumn's head, and she sat contentedly in front of her mother, playing with a bright yellow sponge duck while Lorraine massaged her head and created silly shapes with her shampooed hair.

Mother and daughter talked and laughed, oblivious to the camera's invasion. Lorraine's nipples peeked out above the rich bubbles, her breasts moving in a tantalizing sway with each motion of her arms.

Dan could never watch without becoming aroused. His response wasn't simply a physical reaction to Lorraine's body, however; it was to the intimacy of the scene. It came from the knowledge that this precious woman and child were his. The vision unerringly touched him.

The sound of water squeezed from the duck echoed in the small room. Dan watched, transfixed as always, knowing the exact moment Autumn would notice him.

"Daddy!"

"Tom," Lorraine admonished, a wondering smile on her shiny-clean face. "How long have you been there?"

"My hair's gonna have body and—and what, Mommy?" Autumn turned her soapy head to glimpse her mother's face.

"And manageability," Lorraine supplied. "That's what the bottle says, anyway."

"And managerility," Autumn predicted. "I'll be as pretty as Mommy, won't I?"

"You are as pretty as Mommy." Dan's voice came from behind the camera.

"Our water's getting cold, we'd better rinse you." She waggled sudsy fingers at Dan. "'Bye."

"Go right ahead, you're not bothering me," he teased.

She took the water-soaked duck from Autumn and hefted it. The camera lens careened across the ceiling and the cabinets for several seconds while Dan dodged the sponge, amidst laughter and water splashing. In the next shot Lorraine reached across the bathroom for a towel, water sluicing down her glistening body. Then she reached him, and the film stopped.

Gray and white spots dotted the screen. He'd never taped anything else on the cassette. Dan flicked it off with the remote at the same time he saw Lorraine standing a few feet away, holding her purse. A network program came on and he turned the volume down and sat up. "I didn't know you were home."

"Got here a few minutes ago." She sat her purse inside the closet and kicked off her shoes. She wore a short flowered sundress with a little white T-shirt underneath, enhancing her tan and her slim legs and arms.

"How was the movie?" he asked.

"Good. It was nice to relax. How were the girls?"

"Great. They play so well together. Maybe we should have tried for another girl, after all."

She tossed him a tolerant glance. "Yeah, right. More likely we'd have had another wild set of boys." She grabbed a nightshirt and went into the bathroom. A few minutes later, she returned and pulled down the rumpled comforter. Her hair had been brushed and fell in waves around her shoulders. "I forgot about that video."

Without reply, he handed her the remote and propped himself against the headboard with a pillow behind his shoulders.

"I thought maybe you'd taped over it."

"Nope."

A few minutes later, she picked up a book from the night table.

"I get a woody every time I watch it," he admitted.

Abruptly, she sat up and aimed the book at his head.

Dan knocked it aside with one wrist and reached for her. Lorraine laughed and tried to roll away, but he pinned her beneath one leg and half his chest.

She didn't try to escape. Instead, she looked up at him with eyes as pure as twenty-four-karat gold, a smile gracing lips he knew were warm and soft and oh-so-kissable.

Dan framed the side of her face with one hand and caught his fingers in her tumbled mass of hair. "I want you to be my wife again," he said, all playfulness removed from his tone. "Not just pretend this time. I mean marry me. For real."

She tried to turn her head, but he didn't let her.

"You don't have to say anything right now. I know you love me. I know what we have together—what we had all those years together was real, even if the law says it's not legal. You're my wife."

Her eyes glistened brightly in the lamplight as she fought tears.

"Just think about it. And think about the alternatives."

She frowned and, quick as lightning, her gold eyes darkened to gemlike topaz. Lorrie's heart pounded erratically. "What alternatives?"

His hold on her relaxed. "We could—" He paused. "I could tell everyone."

Lorrie'd imagined it a hundred times. She dreaded anyone knowing the truth, and could only guess at the reactions. The children finding out disturbed her most.

"You could leave me," he said, his voice flat. "Or kick me out. We wouldn't need a divorce."

Hearing him say it, hearing his words and his voice make it reality, pierced her heart to its very core. He allowed her to turn to her side and bury her face in the sheet.

"Is that what you want, Lorraine?" he asked, his lips in the crook of her neck.

She shook her head and drew her fist to her mouth.

"Or..." he said, kissing her neck, her ear and her jaw, sending a tremor of need and desperation through her body, "we could go back to what we were—two people who love each other."

She wanted that more than anything. If only it were that simple.

"I want to be with you." His voice was gruff against her ear. "I want us to be together. If that's what you want, too, please help me decide what to do."

"You want me to tell you what to do, that's what you want."

"No. I need help. I need to know what you're thinking and feeling."

She turned to face him then, something about his broken plea penetrating her hurt and humiliation, and slid her arm around his neck. "I want to forgive you," she said almost angrily. "I want things to be like they were before, and I don't know how to do either one of those things."

He touched his forehead to hers. "I know."

"Sometimes I almost forget," she confessed. "When we're working at the barns or when I'm just going about my daily chores. I forgot for a little while tonight."

Dan stroked her shoulder.

"And then I remember. It comes back to me and this sick, sinking feeling hits my chest and I'm jerked into reality. I want to share it with you. I want to come to you and tell you how I'm feeling, and then I remem-

ber, you're the one who brought it all on, and I get mad
all over again.''

"It's okay," he said. "You can be mad at me. You
can be mad. Just don't stop loving me. Don't shut me
out anymore."

She ran her fingers through the hair at his temple and
he moved his head back to look at her. "Okay," she
said.

He gave her a quick, urgent kiss. "Okay. We'll figure it out together, then?"

She nodded.

Relief relaxed his features visibly.

He was right. The alternatives were unthinkable.
They had to come up with something that would pre-
serve their family, their relationship, and help Tom.
And right now Lorrie didn't have a clue what that might
be.

"Hey, Uncle Buzz!" Thad called from the open
doorway of the tractor barn.

"Hi, guys. What're you doin'?"

His brother laid a wrench on the concrete with a clang
and glanced up. "Trying to get this bike running
again," he said. "What have you been up to?"

"Not much," he replied, approaching. "I'm enjoying not seeing that crowd of cars down at the barns."
On the weekends, the parking lot had been full and vehicles had even parked along the highway.

His twin, grease streaked up one forearm to his elbow and a rag jutting from the hip pocket of his faded
jeans, hunkered beside the moped and studied the motor intently.

Another scene superimposed itself over the sight of
his brother and nephew, another day, just as real as this

one: In the open garage doorway, Dan had been squatting beside the black Harley, a spoke wrench in his greasy hands. Tom had walked toward him with an ache in his gut, dreading what he was about to say, what he was about to do.

"Sometimes I want to take the top of your head off and screw your brain in right." Dan had said to him. *"You can't be serious."*

"Never more serious in my life, Danny-boy." He'd said the words aloud. Hadn't he?

"What'd you say?" Dan asked, glancing over his shoulder.

Tom stood, his Nikes welded to the cement drive, while an avalanche of inevitable memories crashed down on him, burying him in a ferocious sense of déjà vu and sending a wave of dizziness across his eyes. He flung his arms out as if to steady himself and took a few awkward steps.

"Are you all right?" his brother asked, slowly standing. "Hey, what's the matter?"

Tom blinked and oriented himself. He stared at his twin, noting the scattering of gray hairs along his temple. Thad looked just like him. Just like Dan.

He backed out of the tractor barn and took a good hard look at the outside. The metal building had been extended and painted white. The cement drive was wider and the concrete pad beside the gas pump hadn't been there before.

He surveyed the meadow to his left where their house used to stand. It had been two-and-a-half stories with a sagging front porch and rose bushes climbing the south side. They'd washed up at the old hand pump in the side yard.

He turned and stared.

He knew exactly who he was. He was Thomas Beckett, eldest son of Gil Beckett by three-and-a-half minutes. The man standing in front of him was Daniel. *Daniel.*

"Are you okay?" Dan asked.

Tom gathered his wits. "I just got a little dizzy there."

"Maybe you'd better sit down for a minute."

"I'm okay now."

"You sure?"

"Yeah."

Dan went back to the bike, he and Thad exchanging a light banter as they cleaned the spark plugs and put them back. Tom watched for a while. Dan had always enjoyed working on cycles. He liked the work, getting his hands into the job. Tom, on the other hand, liked where the wheels took him.

"What, you're not offering your expert advice?" Dan asked after time had passed and Tom hadn't spoken.

"You're doing all right," he replied.

"D'ya hear that, Thad? We're doing all right."

What had he walked into? He'd been considering a trip home before his accident. After years of wandering, working in one place after another, he'd settled into a life he enjoyed, met a woman he could love.

Cedra. Tom thought of her back at the house, no doubt sleeping in. He'd met her nearly two years ago, and after six months they'd moved in together. He'd been about to ask her to marry him, but had waited, wondering if he should tell her about his family, if he should come home and make peace, tell them about her—about himself now that he had things straightened out in his head—now that he had his head straightened out.

Maybe not remembering had worked out for the best. Here was Dan pretending to be him and nobody the wiser! What the hell was that all about?

While Dan worked, Tom studied him covertly, noting the subtle ways he'd changed over the years. He remembered nights sleeping in narrow beds side by side, morning after morning taking the school bus together, playing the usual look-alike pranks on anyone and everyone they could fool.

Adolescent years came to mind with less fondness. His dad had harangued him ceaselessly, harping constantly about college and the damned orchards.

It was hard enough looking just like his brother who did everything right. Teachers compared them, relatives compared them, and Gil...Gil wanted Tom to fit the nice, neat mold he'd created. He chipped and chipped and chipped away at Tom's distinctive edges until he knew he'd be a round peg just like Dan if he didn't get the hell away from this place.

So he'd gone. And he'd stayed gone. And no one had missed him, because they didn't realize he was the one who'd left.

"I'll see you later." Tom headed back to the house, his entire outlook changed, his whole world changed. He remembered his life.

He was Thomas Beckett. And he had one up on the rest of the family: He knew he was Thomas Beckett. They didn't realize he'd regained his memory.

He savored the knowledge, keeping it to himself for the time being. Something strange was going on here and he wanted a better understanding before they became aware of his recovery.

Just who-all knew, he wasn't sure. Dan, obviously. And probably Lorrie. No doubt that's where the uneasy vibes he'd picked up on came from. He observed them for days, watched their awareness of one another. Sometimes it seemed they forgot whatever strained their relationship. They'd be sitting at the table or playing with one of the kids, and then a casual touch or a laugh would remind them and their faces would change. The uneasiness was so subtle, Tom was sure none of the others picked up on it.

Tom studied Lorrie one afternoon, as she folded clothes and stacked them on the kitchen table. It had been such a long time ago that they'd dated. He probably could have liked her better—maybe even fallen for her—if Gil hadn't pushed her on him.

But since she'd been his father's choice, she hadn't been his, even though she had appealed to him. Teenage hormones had prevailed, however. After that, he'd gotten scared. Scared of getting trapped. Scared of becoming what his father wanted him to become. Scared of missing out on everything life had to offer.

So he'd left. Taking off hadn't been fair to her. It hadn't been fair to Dan. But life wasn't fair, and he had to live with himself.

Now that he saw her, knew her, he couldn't help wondering what his running out on his unbearable life had done to her. Apparently she hadn't missed him too much because she'd immediately married Dan. Why had she done that?

A dawning possibility made the hair in his neck stand up. Had she been pregnant? He couldn't recall more than maybe one time with her. Rapidly, he tallied Thad's age and tried to remember when Dan had said his birthday was. It was possible. But why would they have pretended that Dan was him? That blew his mind more than anything.

"Did you and Tom go out very long before you got married?" he asked.

Lorrie smoothed a neatly folded T-shirt without looking at him. "Not really. We'd known each other since we were young, though."

He remembered. Gil had dragged him to every boring veterans' shindig, yapping the whole way about the Loring girl and how he should treat her nice and spend time with her. "Did you have a big wedding?"

She shook her head. "Your mother wasn't up to it, and Gil was occupied with taking care of her."

His mother. The memory was like a fall that knocked the wind out of his lungs. The day he left, he'd gone to her bed in the dining room and sat beside her for an hour, holding her hand, telling her his dreams. What he hadn't told her, what he didn't have the courage to tell her, was goodbye.

Like a coward, he'd left that up to Dan.

"When did she die?"

Lorrie looked up at him. "The March after you left." Unthinkingly, she folded the fabric-softener sheet into a square. "I remember it rained lightly the morning of her funeral and cleared off before the service. It turned into a pretty day, with the orchards ready to blossom."

"So, you, after you were married, you moved into the house and took care of her?"

"Not entirely. Your father did most of it. I took over the house. It was in pretty bad shape, what with just the men knocking around in it, needing all their time in the orchards."

So Gil got the daughter-in-law he'd wanted, after all. "And then Thad came along?"

"A couple of weeks after your mother died. I wish she could have seen him."

Tom imagined Dan and Gil and Lorrie going through his mother's things, taking down the bed she'd spent her last days in. A new baby must have been a welcome diversion. "I'll bet it helped Dad, getting a new grandson so soon after she died."

"Thad was good for all of us," she replied.

Tom saw Thad with new eyes, too. He couldn't help wondering. Was Thad his? Was that the discomfort he sensed between Dan and Lorrie? They'd probably felt safe in thinking that Tom wouldn't be back and no one would ever know the difference. And no one would. Hell, how could they? Thad looked just like both of them!

And Gil. Tom observed the old man's frustration at being unable to help Dan. He saw his pride in the orchards, in Dan, in his grandchildren. How hard it must have been for such a proud, unyielding man to care for a bedridden wife, to wonder what would become of the orchards after he himself died. Perhaps seeing his wife's mortality had made his own clear, and he'd taken measures to secure the property and the business for future generations.

Tom wasn't ready to forgive him, but maybe, just maybe, he could understand him a little better.

He was sure Gil didn't know about Dan's masquerade. There would have been no purpose in him instigating it. And certainly no good would have come of Dan telling him. How could Gil have been so blind to the fact that Dan had assumed a new identity?

None of it made sense.

And then there was Cedra....

Having his memory intact where Cedra was concerned was pure torture. Having known her as a stranger these past weeks only made him appreciate her more.

On the outside, she was this fun-loving yet needy, slightly outrageous little sexpot. But Tom knew her on the inside, too. Knew the knocks life had dealt her without scarring her warm heart and her giving nature. Tom hadn't been long out of treatment when he'd met her. He'd been sitting, nursing a Coke at a company Christmas party, when she'd zeroed in on his loneliness and paused in serving drinks to speak with him.

"Can I get you something?" she'd asked, a tray of empty glasses on her hip. Her warm brown eyes took in his hair and skimmed his face.

"Not unless you have a time machine that'll end this party quicker."

"Sorry, I just served the last one." She smiled. "Not having a good time?"

"Oh, it's okay. It's just that . . ."

"What?"

"Nothing." Nearly all the employees had brought a spouse. Those who hadn't were already well on their way to being drunk and disorderly.

Tom had visited with his boss and his wife for a half hour or so, and the next time he saw the little waitress, she brought him a fresh Coke.

"Worked here long?"

"A couple of years. Em is a close friend of mine."

"Em's the owner?"

She nodded. "I tend bar, but tonight I'm filling in for one of the girls." She stuck her free hand out. "I'm Cedra."

"Buzz."

"Nice to meet ya, Buzz."

"You involved, Cedra?"

She shook her head and her silver earrings swung.

"Want to grab a sandwich with me later?"

"I can't leave till one."

"I'll wait."

Her lips had turned up at his words and she'd given him a thoughtful look. "You're on, Buzz."

Meeting Cedra had been worth the wait. Knowing her would have been worth any wait.

School had started that week and the boys were full of tales about kids and teachers and pranks on the school bus. Jori had joined a soccer team, so the family was practicing in the side yard with him.

Tom maneuvered getting on the same team as Cedra, and used every opportunity to touch her, stooping as low as bumping into her and then catching her.

"Buzz, be careful of your arm," she said, laughing.

"My arm's fine," he declared, tightening it around her to show her just how fine.

Her eyes widened. "Buzz..."

"Let's go for a ride tonight," he said so the others couldn't hear.

She blinked.

"All right?"

She gave him a curious look, but she agreed. "All right."

Dan and Lorrie put the kids to bed and Tom saw that Gil was settled in the family room. "Cedra and I are going into town. Don't wait up."

Outside, Tom motioned for Cedra to hand him the keys to her Taurus, got in and rolled the windows down. She climbed in beside him and fastened her seat belt.

She crossed her bare legs, and Tom forced his attention to the road. Fireflies danced in the tall grass along the sides.

"Buzz, you're speeding."

"Uh-huh." The wind tore through his hair and he glanced over to see her short locks in charming disarray. She'd changed into fresh clothes after their soccer game, and wore a short pair of pink-and-white-striped bibs with a formfitting little sport-bra-thing underneath. The effect was as appealing as peppermint candy to a hungry man with a sweet tooth.

She slid one of her Eagles tapes in the player and leaned back in the seat, seductively tapping her red nails on her bare knees.

Tom drove to the Lied Center and careened into a parking spot beneath a light pole. "Wait here a minute."

He ran in and returned ten minutes later, then grabbed a bag he'd tossed in the back. He opened her door.

"What are you doing?"

"I have a surprise for you. Come on."

Chapter 11

With a curious lift of her brows, Cedra swung her legs around and got out. He led her along the well-lit walkway, into the tile-floored lobby, past the registration desk and down a corridor of hotel rooms. The same enormous timbers that stood floor to ceiling in the high-ceilinged lobby stood beside each room's door.

"Where are we going?" she asked.

They came to a set of stairs and Tom led her up and into another hallway. "You'll see."

"I smell a pool. Are we going to swim? I didn't bring a suit."

"Maybe later."

"Buzz—"

He took her hand and pulled her forward, along the corridor, finally stopping to slide a key in a lock.

Cedra stepped inside and surveyed the nicely furnished hotel room. Tom dropped the bag on the floor and moved toward her. She placed her hand against his chest. "What are you doing?"

"What does it look like?" He flattened his palm on her arm and ran it up to her shoulder.

"It looks like you brought me here with an ulterior motive."

Tom slid his thumb under her top near the upper swell of her breast and savored the silky skin he'd been thinking about for days. "It does look like that, doesn't it?"

Her dark eyes took on a sultry glow. "But you said it wouldn't be fair."

He delved his hand into her hair and lowered his face to hers.

"You said it wouldn't be fair to either of us," she objected, less than an inch from his lips.

His other hand slipped up the back of her shorts and discovered the satiny scrap of underclothing beneath. "I remember," he said.

"That you said that?"

"No."

"What do you remember?"

"I remember the way you kiss."

Her sultry, dark eyes widened. "You do?"

He pressed her against his thigh. "I remember your tiny triangle of crisp black curls."

"Oh-h-h..." Her breath rushed out against his chin.

"And I remember how good it feels to sink deep inside you."

Her trembling eyelids drifted closed.

"I remember I love you."

She opened her eyes and framed his cheeks, pushing his face from hers. "Are you just saying this because you know how badly I need to hear it?"

"No."

"You really remember?"

"I do."

"What, then," she demanded, her voice catching. "Tell me what you remember."

"We met when you worked the Christmas party at Em's. We had a sandwich at Denny's and we drank coffee until early in the morning. The next week I called you and we drove to Nashville for a day."

She gaped at him in disbelief.

"The first time we slept together was at my place and you cried afterwards," he went on. "I thought I must have done something wrong, but you told me your past had been so messed up that you didn't think you'd ever meet a man who would make you feel good about yourself."

She cried then, just as she had that night. Huge tears rolled down her cheeks and dripped from her chin. She held his face in both hands and kissed him hard. "You remember! You really remember!"

Tom inched the straps of her shorts from her shoulders until she stood in her tiny top and bikini. She crossed her arms, elbows pointing at him and tugged the top over her head. "You have too many clothes on," she said, her voice a husky promise.

Tom took care of the problem in a heartbeat while she stripped the spread from the bed and knelt in the middle.

"I've missed you, Cedra." He joined her, running his fingers over her skin, brushing her dark, swollen nipples.

"I've missed you." She rose on her knees and he joined her, their bodies touching in an arousing first taste of the pleasure to come.

He kissed her, remembering why he loved her, why she'd become the woman he needed and wanted. He kissed her, knowing he had to say the next words before anything else passed between them. "I want to marry you."

Her breath fanned his lips. Her heart thudded against his chest. She tightened her fingers on his shoulder.

"Cedra?"

"Yes."

"Will you marry me?"

"Yes."

And like the first time, she cried afterward.

Cedra's bed hadn't been slept in, Lorrie noted when she dressed Autumn that morning. Usually, they tiptoed around, letting her sleep, but today Lorrie took extra time with Autumn's hair and they giggled over silly girl things. Either Cedra hadn't come back last night or she'd gotten up awfully early, and Lorrie highly doubted that.

"Where's Uncle Buzz?" Jori asked at breakfast.

"He must have gotten up early this morning," Dan said. He and Lorrie exchanged a glance that included Gil.

"This crap doesn't even melt into my toast," the old man complained, as if he hadn't noticed.

"Get over it, Dad," Dan said in exasperation. He slammed the butter dish on the table. "There. Eat that if you want to. Clog up those arteries you just got cleared out. Have another heart attack. It's your body and it's your life."

Dan stomped out the door.

The children looked at their mother. "Get rolling, boys," she said. "The bus will be on our road in three minutes. Grab your bags."

Gil looked up. "I was just making conversation."

Lorrie waved her sons out the door and returned to the table with a cup of coffee. Autumn finished her cereal and skipped off to watch her morning cartoon.

"It's hard for him to hear how unhappy you are with your diet. And we know you're frustrated that you can't do as much as before, but there are still plenty of things you can do."

She didn't think he'd answer. He wasn't one to admit his feelings or talk things out. "Like what?" he finally asked.

"Spend time with the kids. Tell them your stories about your parents, about the grandmother they never knew. Grandparents give children a sense of family and belonging. You can share things with them that no one else can."

"I taught that husband of yours everything I know about growing apples."

"I know you did."

"But he learned more at college than I ever knew in the first place."

"I don't think so."

"And he studies, too," he went on. "That's how he got interested in that fancy hybrid stuff he works on with the university. He's a smart boy."

Lorrie had to smile at his reference to Dan as a boy. "Well, you gave him his love for the orchards," she said. "Maybe one of our kids will love them, too."

"I hoped Thad would," he said, the past tense the first she'd heard him admit maybe it wouldn't happen.

"It might not be Thad." Lorrie took a sip from her cup. "Maybe it'll be Bram." She smiled. "Or Autumn."

"Maybe I want to live long enough to see that," he said and took a bite of his now-cold toast with the unmelted, pale spread.

Lorrie grinned. Too bad Dan hadn't stuck around. She couldn't wait to tell him about this conversation. He wouldn't believe it.

"We won't have to do that too many more times. A few more weeks and we can get the pool ready for winter." Dan had come up from the barns and found Lorraine cleaning the pool in her suit and a pair of shorts. Dan observed the wavy white distortion of her legs and feet through the water and watched her sweep the vacuum attachment across the bottom of the pool.

"What do you think Tom and Cedra are doing?" she asked.

"Probably doing the wild thing and not giving a moment's thought to calling us." He perched on the deck, slipped off his boots and socks, rolled up the legs of his jeans, and stuck his feet in.

"Do you really think so?" she asked. "Tom doesn't even remember who she is."

"So you think he's changed? From what I remember, he doesn't have a real big conscience in that department."

She didn't look him in the eye and a blush tinged her cheeks. Dan hadn't meant to embarrass her. He hadn't even been referring to her.

"And she's crazy about him," he went on to cover his blunder. "How long could he resist?"

Lorraine unhooked the vacuum hose and wand, laid them on the deck and waded to where he sat. "Think she's sexy?"

"She's a good kisser."

The evening sun lit her eyes with a sparkle of amusement. God, she was fun. Fun to tease. Fun to love.

"But I prefer my women a little fuller."

Lorraine's brows rose.

"More mature."

"Big mistake, Beckett."

"What—" She grabbed his arm and jerked him into the water beside her. He came up sputtering, his jeans weighing a hundred pounds, his T-shirt plastered to his body. "At least you let me take my boots off."

Lorraine hoisted herself onto her belly on the edge of the pool and grabbed one of his Dingos.

"No, Lorraine, don't, please, I'm sorry. Don't throw it in."

"It's an old pair."

"But they're my favorites. I'll never get a pair to fit the same. I'm sorry. I think you're sexier than any woman alive. I think you're Cindy Crawford and Julia Roberts and Madonna all rolled into one."

She dangled the boot over the water, and he knew better than to lunge for it.

"You think *Madonna's* sexy?" she asked.

"No. I don't know. Actually I never looked close enough to tell."

She laughed out loud and threw the boot onto the deck behind her.

"But if you got one of those bulletproof bras, you'd have her beat," he finished.

She lunged for him and he moved aside and dunked her. "I wasn't going to get my hair wet," she sputtered, surfacing. "Now I'll have to wash it before bed."

"I'll help you. We can sit in the tub and I'll make curly little horns out of your hair with the shampoo."

She wiped water from her eyes and shook her head. "You're hopeless."

An hour or so later, she finished blow-drying her hair and found him stretched out on the bed. "Look," she said. "Body and managerility."

"I'm going to tell them," he said.

"What? Who?"

"Tom. Dad."

Immediately serious, she sat beside him, her brow furrowed. "Are you sure?"

"I can't stand it anymore, Lorraine. You know and you still love me."

Lorrie shook her head, a sick panicky feeling taking over. "I don't know, I just have to wonder what good could come of it. What would it accomplish for you to tell your dad? Think about it!" It frightened her how they could be physically intimate one moment and have this terrifying wall come up between them the next. "You're being selfish."

He sat up, his expression guarded. One minute, they were in complete accord. Then, in the next second, she couldn't fathom what twists his mind had taken.

"You want your dad to know you're the one who stayed and ran the orchards," she accused. "You're tired of Tom getting all the credit. What difference does it make what your father calls you? It's you he appreciates. It's the work you've done that has made the place a success. You know it's you. I know it's you. Why can't that be good enough?"

"*I'm* being selfish?" His tone was incredulous even to his own ears. "*I'm* willing to admit what I've done and bear the humiliation that goes along with it. *You* just don't want to be embarrassed. You don't want your mom and sisters and the teachers at school and the checkout girl at the Country Mart to know you couldn't tell the difference between your fiancé and his brother and married the wrong one!"

He had reduced her nightmarish fears to a matter of vanity. A surge of anger rushed through her limbs and she pushed herself from the bed.

He'd *never* talked to her like this before.

"Haven't you done enough?" Her voice, though a near whisper, cracked. "Haven't you put me through enough hell without adding to it to ease your conscience?" Her body trembled. "If you tell Gil, I swear to you I'll leave. I'll take the kids and I'll go."

She hadn't realized how forcefully she felt it, how sure she was that she didn't want Dan to reveal their secret, until the words were out of her mouth. They were unfair words, manipulative words. She knew exactly how much he feared her ever saying them.

Or ever following through.

His composure slid and she glimpsed the vulnerable core she'd deliberately attacked.

He got to his feet and she backed away.

They stared at each other and a muscle in his jaw twitched.

"You said you wanted to figure this out together," she reminded him, trying to smooth over her rash threat. "What happened to that?"

"All right," he said finally. "You win. I won't tell Dad."

Lorrie regretted what she'd had to do to keep her sanity. But part of the weight eased from her chest.

"But I'm telling Tom."

Telling Tom was fair. Telling Tom was logical. Telling Tom could backfire and have the same results as telling Gil, but somehow she didn't think it would. If it did, *then* she would have to deal with it. "And please. Please show him how important it is to protect the children."

He nodded without looking at her.

"When will you tell him?"

He laid his palm on his chest as if the thought already pained him. "I don't know. Tonight if I have the guts."

They'd said too many hurtful things. Things that had come too painfully close to the truth. They both knew it. They both resented it. Neither was ready to forget.

Dan grabbed his boots and left the room. Lorrie sank to the bed's edge and covered her lips with trembling fingers. Would this nightmare never end? How could it? All she could do was protect her children. And maybe in doing so, she'd salvage a little of her self-respect.

And right now, she needed all the self-respect she could muster.

He found Tom in the tractor garage, the lights blazing to chase off the night, the wrecked Harley a heap of parts. "What are you doing?"

Tom glanced up. "This isn't as bad as it looked. The frame's good. The exhaust is toast, a lot of the chrome too, but it can be fixed."

Dan inspected the parts his brother had removed. "I wish I could say the same about my life," he thought aloud.

Tom set the wheels aside. "Trouble in Blissville?"

"Bigger than trouble."

Tom pulled up a couple of wooden crates. "Park it and tell me."

It seemed like such a natural thing to do, Dan didn't think twice. He sat and watched Tom take off the gas tank. Neither of them spoke for long minutes, but the silence was comfortable.

Finally, Dan worked up the courage. His heart tripped against his shirtfront. "There's something I have to tell you."

"Shoot."

"There's no good way to say it. It can't be softened or hedged."

Tom looked up.

Now or never. Dan swallowed. "I've been lying to you."

His brother's glance darted uncomfortably back to the wrench in his hand.

"Years ago. Before you left, you were seeing Lorraine. Dad wanted the two of you to get married. He kind of pushed you that way and her father pushed her. I—I had always had a crush on her. Way back when Dad took us to the Legion Hall. I guess maybe I was even jealous that you were the one she paid attention to. 'Course you were better at stuff than I was. You made friends easier. People liked you."

This was turning into more of a confession than Dan had planned. But he couldn't tell Tom the truth without telling him why.

"Anyway, when you decided to leave, you came and told me. I gave you my bike. This bike."

Tom still didn't raise his head.

"You left me with the job of telling Dad and Lorraine that you'd gone. I sat for hours trying to figure out how to do that." Dan let silence stretch between them for several minutes before he went on. "What this boils down to is that I didn't tell them you'd gone. When Lorraine came looking for you, I asked her to marry me. And I told her *I* had gone. I married her, pretending to be you. You're not Dan. You're Tom."

Dan waited for an explosion. He'd prepared himself for resentment. For shock and disbelief. For a hundred questions. He'd been unfair to Tom ever since his arrival. Anger would have been normal.

Finally Tom raised his head. If Dan hadn't known better, he'd have thought the look behind his eyes was guilt of his own.

"I know," was all he said.

Confusion clouded Dan's comprehension. "What?"

"I know who I am. I just didn't know why you were calling yourself by my name."

Dan gaped at him, stunned. "You know? You know who you are?"

Tom nodded.

"Then why the hell didn't you let on?"

Tom shrugged. "I've just been biding my time, trying to figure out what was going on."

"How long have you known?"

"Just this week. I remembered the day you and Thad were fixing the moped."

"And you never let on."

"I was too confused. I finally remembered who I was, and there you were going around as me. Not exactly your average situation."

Dan shook his head.

"I guess I get it now," Tom said. "You were in love with Lorrie all along?"

"I must have been."

"So you thought if you pretended you were me, you'd have her."

"It worked."

"What did you think would happen if I ever came back?"

"I stayed awake nights afraid of that," Dan admitted.

"And then I finally did come back, but I didn't remember who I was." He gave a sharp, humorless laugh.

Outside locusts droned. Tom laid the wrench on the concrete.

"There's one thing I have to know," he said.

Dan agreed.

"Who is Thad's father?"

So he'd thought of that, had he? The fact that he had to wonder hit Dan with a pang like a punch in the gut.

"I am." Saying the words gave him immense satisfaction.

Tom's deep blue eyes assessed his as though searching for the truth. "And Lorrie?"

Dan looked at him.

"She knows now?"

"She knows. I told her after you showed up."

Tom exhaled a deep gust of breath. "Man. She never suspected?"

"No."

"How did she take it?"

Dan stood. He paced a few feet away and back, raking his fingers through his hair. "Just like you'd think. At first she couldn't believe it. And then she got mad.

She's mad. She's hurt. She's betrayed. She's ashamed. She has a right to everything she's feeling.''

"What a mess."

Dan stopped beside him.

"I feel..." Tom glanced up, then away. "Partly to blame."

It was Dan's turn to emit a wry laugh. "You didn't have a clue what I did after you left. How can you be to blame?"

"I left. I left everything and everyone in the lurch. I even expected you to explain to Mom for me."

"You do owe me for that one," Dan pointed out.

"Dan."

Hearing his name brought a sharp sting to his eyes. He inspected the metal crossbeams overhead. "Yeah."

"I'm sorry."

Dan struggled with his emotions. "I'm the one who should be saying he's sorry."

"All right."

Dan shot Tom a glance and saw he wore a grin.

"I think I owe you an explanation, too," Tom said.

"I know why you left."

"You know how it was with Dad. You don't know the rest of it."

Feeling more at ease, Dan settled back on the crate.

"I had a drug problem," Tom said bluntly.

Dan tried to take in his words.

"Oh, I didn't think so at the time," he went on. "After high school and my attempt at college I was still having a good time. Experimenting. Thinking I had a handle on my life. Dad was my problem. This place was my problem. You," he said, gesturing with a greasy hand, "were my problem. I could have quit any time I wanted. I just didn't want to."

Dan absorbed the confession, but a layer of shock kept it from completely sinking in.

"It wasn't until later. A long time later, when I was doing hard stuff, that I realized it had control of me. I couldn't keep a job. Couldn't keep a woman." He turned to the bike strewn across the floor. "This is the only thing I ever hung on to."

As many times as Dan had imagined his brother's life away from here, he'd never imagined it as Tom described it to him now.

"The day I polished it and took it for an estimate so I'd have money to get high, was the day I knew I had to get help. Instead of taking the money for the bike, I rode it to a treatment center in Texas and checked myself in. One of the counselors kept it in his garage for me until I got out."

"I wish I'd known," Dan said helplessly.

"I worked my way back north. When I met Cedra in Tennessee, I stayed longer than I'd stayed anywhere before. Got my own place, started saving. She knew that part about me. Somehow it's easier to tell people you're an addict than to tell them you ran out on a dying mother and a father who needed your help."

"Tom, I—I..." He couldn't even think of a response.

"But now you know...you know why I didn't come back all that time."

"It's hard knowing," Dan told him, honestly.

After a minute, Tom asked, "What are you going to do now?"

Dan shrugged. "Lorraine won't let me tell Dad the truth."

"I can understand that."

"What about Cedra? Does she know you have your memory back?"

"She knows. I didn't tell her I'm really Tom, though. I figured there's time for that."

"I've asked Lorraine to marry me." The words sounded funny. He'd gone through the ceremony once, lived with her as man and wife ever since, yet he'd had to ask her again.

Tom looked perplexed, too.

"We're not really married," he explained. "Because I used your name on the license."

"*I'm* not married to her then, am I?"

Dan almost laughed. "No."

"Well, what about—"

His question was cut off by a scream coming from the direction of the house. Dan sat up straight. Not a scream like one of the kids playing; it was too late for that anyway.

He heard it again. A sound of pure terror. Rising, he knocked over the crate and tore out of the garage.

"Da-a-an!" Screams pieced the air from the direction of the house. "Da-a-an!" Was that Lorraine? The outdoor lights were on, illuminating the redwood fence and the deck. Water splashed and a woman sobbed.

Dan ran through the open gate and up the stairs to where Lorraine, in a drenched nightgown, knelt over a small figure and sobbed.

The acrid smell of vomit met his nostrils at the same time he saw his tiny daughter lying limp on the deck, her hair and pajamas plastered to her pale skin.

Autumn.

Chapter 12

The scene came into focus, and horror like he'd never known slammed into his skull. Ignoring the nauseating smell and Lorraine's near-hysteria, Dan assessed Autumn's unconscious condition and knelt beside her.

"She's not breathing. Oh, my God, oh, my God," Lorraine sobbed beside him. "Oh, Autumn, baby. Baby, oh, this is my fault."

Sensing Tom's presence, Dan glanced past her overwrought face and discovered his brother's tense one. "Call 9-1-1," he ordered.

Tom took off like a shot.

Dan tried to remember his shaky CPR training, telling himself calmness was the first priority. Calmness would have been a whole lot easier if it hadn't been his daughter lying here, if Lorraine wasn't in a state of alarm, and if he remembered what to do. But he had no choice. The paramedics at the rescue station were miles away and there was no telling how long Autumn hadn't been breathing.

Someone had to act quickly.

He placed his fingers beneath her chin and felt for a pulse. Nothing. He leaned down and placed his ear against her nose. Nothing. He glanced at her lifeless face. She had a translucent blue lump on her forehead near her hairline.

After clearing her mouth with his finger, he tipped Autumn's head back to clear the airway, remembering that much from watching videos and practicing on a dummy. Dan pinched her nose, covered her mouth with his and blew. Two quick breaths for a kid, wasn't it? How hard was appropriate for a four-year-old? Could he hurt her?

"She threw up all that water, why doesn't she breathe?" Lorraine asked in a voice that trembled, but had gained more control.

Through her soaked pajamas, Dan felt Autumn's chest for the appropriate place, covered it with the heel of his hand and pressed. Vaguely he recalled that it was unlikely to actually break any ribs, but still he was afraid to push too hard. "Keep count, Lorraine. That's two."

She obeyed. "Three. Four. Five."

He moved back to Autumn's mouth and breathed for her. Two quick ones and back to her chest for five palpitations. He repeated the process again and again.

Lorraine lost count to sob for seconds before she got herself under control again.

Tom knelt on Autumn's other side. Vaguely, Dan realized the boys had come onto the balcony above and one of them was crying. "Let me take a turn, Dan," Tom said gently.

Dan kept count for Tom, watched him breath into Autumn's mouth. It was easier doing it himself: he didn't have to think as much. An eternity passed. Cedra brought a robe for Lorraine, urged her away from the men, and held her trembling shoulders.

Finally, sirens broke through the stillness of the night. Dan knew all three volunteer paramedics who showed up.

"You've got a pulse," Rob Welch said.

"Why isn't she breathing?" With his hands on his knees, Dan watched.

"You've been breathing for her," he replied. "She'll do it on her own in a second here."

Dan stood and backed away, grateful to let those who knew what they were doing attend to Autumn. He ran his hand through his hair and stared at the dark heavens, praying silently.

"There we go," one of them said, finally.

"She's breathing," Rob announced.

Hope surged into Dan's chest. The paramedics moved Autumn into the back of the ambulance, checking her vital signs, and placing an oxygen mask over her face. Her eyes were still closed and she still lay without moving. Dan followed the attendants, Lorraine clinging to his side, her body shaking.

"This is my fault," she said. "I didn't make sure the gate was locked."

Dan cupped her face hard and forced her to look at him. "I came through that gate, too. It could have been either of us."

"I didn't finish putting things away after I cleaned the pool. I always put them away and check the gates."

"Enough," he said. "Guilt isn't going to help her."

Lorraine's wide, luminous eyes were filled with fear and remorse.

"She's stable. We're moving. You comin'?" Rob prepared to close the back doors of the rescue unit.

Lorrie glanced down at her damp robe and bare feet.

"We're coming." Dan turned to his brother. "Bring Lorraine some clothes, will you? Cedra, find them for him and then stay with the boys."

Cedra nodded.

Tom waved them off, and Dan and Lorrie climbed into the back of the ambulance. The siren wailed and Lorrie jumped.

"Is she all right?" Lorrie asked, studying her daughter's pale face. A little color had returned to her blue lips.

"Her heart rate's good and she's breathing on her own."

"I was just falling asleep and thought I heard a splash," she said. "I didn't think much of it. It was like part of my dream or something. I thought I heard someone call me." She looked up at Dan and gripped her own elbows, trying to stop the shaking. "I sat up and waited a few minutes, without hearing anything. I felt like I should go turn on the deck light and look outside. When I did, I saw something in the pool and . . . and I realized . . ."

Lorrie could hardly finish, remembering her horror at recognizing the small, still figure of her child floating on the surface.

". . . I realized it was Autumn. I fell going down the stairs." She pulled the robe away from her shin and revealed a bloody scrape. "I didn't feel this till just now."

With gloved hands, Rob opened an antiseptic packet and handed her the cloth. "Better clean it."

Lorrie sat holding the cool pad between her shaking fingers. "I'm not sure how long she was actually in the water. Can you tell...how can you tell...?" She didn't even want to say it, but she had to know. "Will they test her at the hospital? To see if she has any brain damage?"

"Not right away. You'll have to wait for her to wake up."

Absently, Lorrie noticed that Dan had taken the cleansing pad from her hand and wiped her leg clean. "I couldn't bear for anything to be wrong with her. I'd lose my mind if I thought—"

"Lorraine." Dan placed his fingers over her lips to silence her. "Hush. Please."

The tone of his voice reminded her of their argument. Of the things she'd said to him. Her life was a mess. She pulled her robe close around her and rode in silence the rest of the way to the hospital.

It was the longest night of her life.

Lorrie huddled on a padded vinyl chair and sipped lukewarm coffee. Bless Cedra for thinking to toss a sweatshirt in a bag, along with jeans, underwear, socks, loafers and her purse. Never mind the sweatshirt was Dan's and two of her could have fit in it; she'd finally stopped shaking.

She watched him walk to the window and stare out through the blinds for the hundredth time. The orange light of dawn bathed the hospital room in an otherworldly light, giving Dan's dark hair a bloodred sheen. The blinds cast horizontal stripes across his sharp features and wide shoulders.

He turned back.

Lorrie met his night-wearied eyes.

He looked away and paced to the side of Autumn's bed. She looked so tiny lying beneath the white blanket, a blinking light on a monitor the only reassuring sign that her heart was strong and steady. Dan glanced at Lorrie again, and quickly away.

She couldn't blame him for looking away. She wouldn't blame him for never wanting to look at her or talk to her again. She wouldn't blame him if he hated her.

The doctor said he'd saved Autumn's life.

She'd sat there blubbering and he'd breathed life into their baby. At the moment, Lorrie couldn't even stand her own company. She bit her knuckle and refused to cry.

Dan said it wasn't her fault, but she was responsible. Maybe it was just a mother's lot to experience guilt. She'd gone over it and over it. If only she'd thought to check the gates before they'd gone in. If only she'd gone back out after their bath. If only she'd checked on Autumn.

Why hadn't she had the sense to do exactly what Dan had done? Each time she relived the scene, pictured him kneeling over Autumn, efficiently filling her lungs with air, making her heart beat, she wanted to throw herself at his feet in gratitude and beg him to forgive her.

To think she'd used that very child against him! The memory of how she'd bullied him by threatening to take his children away filled her with such self-disgust that she wanted to bury her head.

And for what? To save face in this town? She'd gladly go down to the Country Mart right now—march into Mercer's Hardware—or run into the American Legion Hall and announce to everyone within hearing distance

that she'd married Dan Beckett, thinking he was Tom—
if it would assure her that her child would be all right.

Lorrie cupped her hand over her mouth and held
back the groan of regret and misery that threatened to
tear from her heart and throat.

Dan stared down at Autumn's pale face. He'd never
seen her so still, so inanimate. Even in sleep, she smiled
and sighed and flung her arms and legs in all directions. The bump on her head had turned a vivid pur-
ple, and the doctor assured them swelling on the outside
was better than swelling on the inside, even though it
looked scary.

She was breathing on her own. Her heart was beat-
ing steadily. All they could do was wait for her to wake
up. He'd only been this scared once before in his life,
and that had been when Lorraine had given birth to
Autumn. It had been touch and go for a while, and Dan
had been terrified at the thought of losing Lorraine.

Losing her had always been a distinct possibility, now
that he thought back on their relationship. But now he
realized something for the first time. As long as she and
the children were alive and well, as long as he knew they
were safe and cared for, he could bear anything.

A tap sounded on the door and Lorraine's mother
and sister entered the room.

"The nurse said it was all right to come in." Ruby's
attention wavered to the child in the bed and she hurried over.

At the sound of soft crying, Dan turned. Lorna had
knelt in front of Lorraine and taken her in her arms.
Good. Someone strong to comfort her. Someone who
wouldn't terrify her more by breaking down and crying
harder than she did.

"Do you have any idea how this happened?" Ruby asked.

Dan turned back to the bed and shook his head.

With age-speckled hands, she petted the hair away from Autumn's bruised forehead. "She must have fallen."

He nodded. "Must have. She's a good swimmer."

"Has she ever sleepwalked? Lorna used to do that. Scared the daylights out of me."

"Not that I know of."

"Maybe she'd be better off in an Omaha hospital," Ruby said.

"I asked about that," Dan replied. "They'd be doing the same things there that they are here. There's really no reason to move her. Unless they decide later that she needs a specialist or something."

They looked at one another over Autumn's still form. Ruby lifted the little girl's hand and held it tenderly. "She just needs some rest. She'll be just fine after she rests. After we visit, I'm going out to the house to help with the children."

"Thanks, Ruby. I know Lorraine will feel better knowing you're with them."

"I'll feel better, too. Like I'm doing something to help."

He understood that need only too well. This helplessness was hell.

"You're going to have to sleep," Dan said to Lorraine late the next evening. She'd eaten a few bites of the sandwich he'd brought her and hadn't said more than a word or two since her mother and sister had been there that morning.

"What about you?"

"We'll take turns. The nurse said she'd have a cot sent up for us."

"You go first," she said.

He saw no point in arguing with her. She was an adult. They both needed to get some rest, and he wasn't foolish enough to think standing here hovering over Autumn was going to help her recover any faster. "All right."

A young male hospital employee in green pants and a loose white jacket wheeled in a folding bed and snapped it open. Dan thanked him. He couldn't tell the difference between doctors and nurses and aides any more. They all dressed casually and wore tennis shoes. He pulled his boots off and laid down, arranging the sterile-smelling white sheet and closing his eyes.

At first, at the sounds of the nurses in the hall and the intercom system, he feared he wouldn't be able to sleep. But what seemed like hours later, voices drifted to him and he came alert.

"We thought it'd be best if we send the boys to school in the morning." His brother's voice, though soft, carried to Dan. "You know, try to keep things as normal for them as we can."

"That's probably a good idea," Lorraine replied. "Are they okay?"

"They're fine. Bram and Jori haven't been bickering. I guess that shows they're upset. Thad helped me with a few chores today."

"And Gil?"

"I'm making him rest. Your mom fusses over him and he's eating up the attention."

"That's Mom."

"She's great." A pause. "How about Dan, is he okay?"

The silence reverberated with Lorraine's shock over Tom's use of Dan's name. Dan lay silent, waiting for one of them to say something.

"Yeah. I know," Tom said finally.

A minute passed. "He told you?"

"He told me. But I already knew. I remembered on my own."

"So, you—you know who you are? You've got your memory back?"

Tom must have nodded.

"Oh, Tom, that's wonderful. I mean, I'm happy for you, that you're all right." A minute later, she said, "He told you what he did?"

"Yeah."

"Were you mad?"

Dan listened, wondering if he should let them know he was awake.

"Mad? No. It would be pretty small of me to have any bad feelings for Dan."

"But he used your name—your identity. Don't you have any feelings about that?"

Dan should have put a stop to their conversation, but he wanted to hear Tom's reply.

"I think I know why he did it. And I'm sorry I placed him in that position. But I understand why you're mad, Lorrie."

"I resent this whole damned mess we're in because of it," she said.

"What about me?" Tom asked. "Don't you resent me?"

Down the hall, a door closed. The sound of shoes squeaked past the doorway and disappeared.

"I should, shouldn't I?" she asked thoughtfully.

"Yeah, you should."

Dan's heart thudded in his chest as if it was going to explode.

"While we're putting all this crap on the table," Tom said, "I want to say I'm sorry. I couldn't see anything past my own need to get away from here. My leaving was nothing at all against you, Lorrie. It was just me."

"It's years too late to get upset about being jilted," Lorraine said. "I've got a bit much on my mind to care about that."

So she forgave Tom for leaving her. Just like that. Not a whimper. Not a recrimination. Apparently Dan was the only bad guy in this whole stinking mess.

"Actually, Lorrie, I did you a favor. I hope you know that."

"What do you mean?"

"I've seen how crazy in love with you my brother is. Why would he have done something so nuts if he wasn't? And for all your resentment, you have it pretty bad for him, too."

Dan waited for her to deny Tom's words. Or confirm them. Several minutes passed. Finally, she said, "Don't do me any more favors, okay?"

A nurse came in shortly after that, and Dan used the opportunity to act as though she'd awakened him.

Lorrie watched the nurse take Autumn's blood pressure, check the monitor and her IV. "Any change?"

"None."

"I'm going to grab a cup of coffee," Dan said. He and Tom disappeared into the hall.

After the nurse left, Lorrie stood beside the bed for several minutes, watching, praying. Finally she lay down on the narrow bed, still warm from Dan's body, and tried to relax her weary limbs.

If only Autumn would wake up. If only she could go back to before this had happened and do it all over again, differently. If only she could go back fourteen years and curtail this whole miserable situation before it got out of hand.

What if Dan had told her the truth? What would have happened? Would they have ended up together anyway? Or would she have married someone else? Those were questions that would never have answers.

She fell asleep and dreamed she and Autumn were being swept along by a swiftly moving current. Lorrie's feet were so cold she couldn't feel them. She and Autumn became separated and Lorrie made a futile attempt to reach her in the river that had grown as thick and slippery as grease.

"Mommy! Mommy!" Autumn cried, the black substance sucking her down.

Lorrie grabbed a branch overhead and struggled to pull herself out of the mire.

"Mommy! Mommy!"

Lorrie woke with a start. She jerked herself up on the edge of the cot and gazed around, completely disoriented. Her scratchy eyes focused on Autumn in the bed and Dan slumped in the chair beside her.

"Is she . . . ?"

Dan shook his head. "No change."

Lorrie ran a hand through her hair. "How long did I sleep?"

"Hours. It's daytime."

A glimpse at the window confirmed that.

"The doctor came by."

"What did he say?"

"That maybe we should be at home seeing to our other children."

Lorrie tried to comprehend. "Meaning what?"

"Meaning that it's been two days, and maybe we should see to the boys."

"But she could wake up any minute!"

"She could."

Lorrie stood and smoothed her wrinkled clothing. "You don't sound very convinced."

"It's just that we don't know how long it could be."

She fumbled with her purse. Pulling out her brush, she ran it through her tangled hair. "It could be today."

Dan didn't say anything.

"It could be this very minute." She walked to the bed and gripped the side rail, with her brush forgotten in one hand. "Autumn, wake up," she said sternly. "Wake up, do you hear me, you're scaring Mommy."

Dan shared her desperation, felt it to his very bones. He got up and stretched his legs, moving beside her and slipping his arms around her waist. Both parents contemplated Autumn's face hopefully. The blinking red light on the monitor mocked them.

"I'll go," Dan said. "When the boys get home from school I'll be there to answer their questions and have supper with them. When they go to bed, I'll shower and come back."

It was what she should have done. She should have thought of it. Of course the boys were scared and their life had been disrupted. They needed reassurance. They needed their parents. Dan would know what to say. He'd know how to handle everything. Feeling woefully inadequate, Lorrie reassured herself with the fact that Dan was taking care of things. "I'll call if there's any change."

He merely nodded. Of course she would call if there was a change. That's what this vigil was all about, wasn't it? She'd really wanted to say, "Thank you. I'm sorry."

Instead, she watched him go.

Dan stood in the shower, hands braced against the tiles, steaming water piercing his face and shoulders. Spending the evening with the boys had been good for all of them. Tom and Cedra had slipped off and left them alone for an hour or so. Bram and Jori had needed reassurance and hugs. Thad, seeming far older than his thirteen years, had done his best to reassure Dan.

At bedtime Dan had sat with each of them individually, had told them he loved them. No matter how many times he said it to them, it would never be enough.

When was the last time he'd told Autumn he loved her? The morning of her accident? The night before? He'd tell her when he got back to the hospital. Maybe she could hear everything they were saying. Or was that just for patients in comas?

Against his will, Dan's mind wandered back over the events of the past days, back to the first moment when he'd seen Autumn's lifeless body on the deck, back to Lorraine's terrified screams.

It came to him then, while the water pounded on his skin, while he dared not cry for fear he'd never stop, that it had been his name Lorraine had cried in her panic. His own name. *Dan.*

He twisted the faucet handle to Off and sluiced water from his hair with his hands. Opening the glass door, he grabbed a towel and stepped out into the steam-filled room. With two swipes, he wiped the wide mirror and stared at his dripping reflection.

Dan.

In her mind, he was Dan now.

From the other room, the phone rang. He wrapped the towel around his waist and grabbed the receiver on the second ring. "Hello."

"It's me." He hadn't often heard Lorraine's voice over the phone. It sounded strangely quiet.

"Is everything okay?"

"She's—awake."

Relief swelled in Dan's chest. He sank to the edge of the bed, ignoring the wet towel around his hips. "Thank God," he breathed.

"She..."

"What?" he asked, sudden fear gripping his lungs, making it hard to breathe. "Is she all right? Lorraine?"

"She has some problems. They've called for her doctor."

Dear God, what now? "I'm on my way."

Chapter 13

The rain that pummeled Nebraska City's tree-lined streets seemed appropriate for the dark thoughts accompanying Dan on his way to the hospital. Thunder rattled the heavens as he parked the Ram and ran toward the door. Inside, fluorescent lighting kept the dismal day at bay, but did nothing for the fear that weighed down his heart.

Dan ran up the stairs and the nurse on duty greeted him. He arrived in Autumn's room out of breath. Lorraine rose from the chair, glanced at Autumn's sleeping face and pointed to the door. Dan took a minute to stand beside Autumn before he followed Lorraine back out into the hall.

"What's wrong?" he asked. "Didn't the doctor come?"

He'd never seen her face so grim. Her normally bright eyes were dull and she held her mouth in a solemn line. "He was here."

"What's wrong?" he asked again.

"She woke up," she said quietly. "I couldn't believe my eyes. She even said my name."

"So she's conscious?"

"Yes. I called for the nurse. Autumn sounded kind of funny, not herself, and she asked for a drink. The nurse was there by then, and she said it was okay, so she got a pitcher of water and a cup and I poured some. Autumn couldn't hold on to the glass." Lorraine's voice quivered. "It slipped and spilled and we had to change her into a dry gown. She couldn't help with that much, either. I ended up having to work her hands through the holes for her."

"Was it because she wasn't fully awake?"

"No, it's not like that. It's like she's younger or something."

Dan looked at her curiously.

"The doctor came and examined her. He's waiting to talk to us together."

"Where?"

"He said to have the nurse page him to the consultation room down the hall."

Dan strode toward the nurses' station.

Several minutes later, they sat on chairs in a tiny, harshly lit room. Dr. Crowley, their family physician, dressed in a casual shirt and slacks, sat across from them.

"Autumn is completely alert and out of any danger," he told them.

"Lorraine says she has a problem, though," Dan said.

"It seems her motor control has been affected slightly. The problem is minor, considering the lack of oxygen to her brain for an extended period. Not only did you save her life, Tom, you prevented any worse brain damage by getting oxygen to her. Her speech is unaffected, she has bladder control. She's remarkably well.''

''What about this motor-control thing? That sounds serious to me.''

''We'll be running a few tests, and I want to call a specialist in from Omaha. It will be a referral, so your insurance will take care of it.'' He glanced from one of them to the other. ''I'm convinced that with some physical therapy she's going to be back to normal in no time. Maybe a couple of months, maybe even sooner. It'll depend on the therapy program, too—whether you bring her in a few times a week or if you take her to the university for a stay. There are even therapists who will come to your home. I'm not sure what your insurance covers, but you could make a call and find out.''

Dan nodded. Autumn was alive. She was fine. A few months of physical therapy were a small price to pay for having their child spared.

''We'll know more after Dr. Demarco sees her in the morning, too. I'm going to keep her until then. After he sees her and gives his prognosis, you can take her home.''

They rose, and Dan shook Dr. Crowley's hand. ''Thanks for coming so late.''

The doctor smiled. ''My wife is used to my hours.''

Dan led Lorraine back to Autumn's room. Autumn turned her head when they entered. ''Daddy!''

Overwhelmed at seeing her awake and hearing her cry his name, Dan stepped to the side of the bed and leaned over to hug her. Her IV had been removed and she wrapped both arms around his neck with unnatural awkwardness. Dan buried his face in the silky hair at her neck and struggled for composure. "Hi, munch-kin."

She kissed his cheek and raised her hand to touch his face. Her hand batted the air for a moment, like a baby's, before she placed her palm against his jaw. "You shaveded."

"Um-hm." He kissed her cheek. "Did you?"

"You silly daddy," she giggled.

He smiled through his tears and kissed Autumn's face soundly.

"My hands are mean," she said.

"They're mean?"

She nodded solemnly. Her four-year-old's vocabulary didn't allow her to express her frustration.

Dan took both of her small hands in his. "Right now they're not minding very well, but they'll get better," he promised.

"Are you mad at me?" she asked, and her eyes, so like Lorraine's, wavered to her mother.

"We're not mad," Lorraine assured her. "We love you very much."

"What were you doing at the pool, Autumn?" Dan asked.

"I thought I lefted my Barbie out there."

"That's why we have rules, Autumn, so you won't get hurt." Lorraine spoke softly.

Autumn's lower lip poked out. "I'm sorry."

"We forgive you, sweetheart." Lorraine reached to fingercomb Autumn's tangled hair from her forehead.

"Nothing is more important than having you safe and all of us being together," Dan added. He told her about the doctor who would be coming to see her.

Lorraine took her to the bathroom, returned and fed her a little orange Jell-O, and Autumn fell asleep.

"Why don't you go home and sleep?" Dan suggested. "I'll stay with her tonight. The doctor won't get here until tomorrow."

Even though she was exhausted, Lorrie couldn't bring herself to leave. Maybe she was being unreasonable, but this was her little girl and she needed to be with her. She shook her head.

Dan didn't argue with her. "I'm gonna call home. Let them know she's okay. They can tell the boys in the morning."

"How were they tonight?"

"As scared as we were. They'll be relieved."

Lorrie nodded. "Call my mom, too, will you?"

"Sure. She can let everyone else know."

Dan left the room and Lorrie lay down on the narrow folding bed. In the back of her mind she noted she was hungry, but bone-tired weariness won her body's attention. She closed her eyes and, within seconds, fell asleep.

Upon Autumn's release from the hospital, the family planned a celebration. Ruby and Lorna invaded the house, cooking and baking up a storm.

Jackie entered the kitchen where the women were gathered. "I'm gonna let Autumn play with my Barbie Big As Me for a whole day."

Lorrie smiled, knowing Autumn had to be eating up all the attention from her brothers and cousin.

"Here, darling." Ruby ushered Lorrie into a chair and placed a glass of orange juice on the table. She opened a cupboard, and Lorrie's eyes widened at the array of vitamins that hadn't been there before.

She swallowed the handful her mother placed in front of her and exchanged a look with Cedra. "Will I need supper?"

Cedra sat beside her. "Sure you will. Your mom spent the afternoon while you were napping showing me how to make noodles."

Lorrie tried not to smile her amusement. She could only imagine Ruby's cooking class and Cedra's reaction. "Sounds great."

"I made radishes into little flowers, too. Wait till you see them."

"I can't wait." Lorrie drank some of her juice.

"Cedra's a natural." Ruby stirred something on the stove. "She's going to make Dan a fine wife."

At Ruby's use of Dan's name, Cedra's eyes met Lorrie's and understanding passed between the two women. Cedra knew Tom was Dan and Dan was Tom. The secret bound them together in a sisterhood all their own. "You're getting married?"

Cedra nodded. "Buzz asked me a few days ago, before I had a chance to tell you."

"That's wonderful." Lorrie leaned and slid her arm around Cedra's shoulder. "I'm really happy for you. And for Buzz."

They exchanged smiles.

Lorrie covered Cedra's hand with her own. "Thanks for being here for the kids that night." Tears welled in her eyes and she blinked them back. "I couldn't even think about what to do or... or anything. But I wasn't worried, leaving them here with you guys."

"I didn't do anything special, Lorrie. I just made them brush their teeth before they went to bed and sat out cereal and bowls in the morning."

"But you were here for them."

"Your mom did the hard stuff—the cooking and laundry."

"Thanks, Mom." Lorrie said.

"No need to thank me," Ruby replied. "That's what mothers are for."

Lorna turned and raised an amused brow at Lorrie.

Lorrie took a deep breath to control her emotions. "I couldn't have made it through any of this without all of you... and..." *Dan,* she'd almost said. "Tom." How she hated calling him that, now that she knew. She hadn't said either name in so long, neither one rolled from her tongue comfortably. "He knew what to do. He saved Autumn's life, you know. And he was so incredibly strong, even though I know he was as scared as I was. I never knew what a strong person he is."

"So are you, Lorrie," her sister said. "I always thought they'd have to knock me out with drugs if something happened to one of my kids. I'd fall apart. But you were a real trouper."

"I guess you don't know until it happens to you," Lorrie answered.

"Well, none of us is ever going to have to find out again," Ruby said firmly. "We've had all the discovery we need."

Amen, Lorrie thought silently.

Gil and Lorrie's father came in the back door just then. "Smells good in here." Orrin noticed Lorrie and stooped to give her a hug. "Hi, hon."

"Dad." She gave him a peck on the cheek.

"We're using the dining room," Ruby announced. "The leaves are in the table. Lorna and Cedra, you set the plates and silverware."

Lorrie got up and helped, happy to be doing normal, useful things in her own home. The warm cooking smells, the banter among the men and women, the familiarity swept away all the pain and confusion of the past weeks and soothed her.

The dining-room table had never been so full of food and family. As her loved ones gathered, she surveyed the smiling faces, Dan on one side of her, Autumn on the other, and a sense of security pervaded her heart. From the head of the table, Dan asked the blessing, his voice deep with emotion on a special word of thanks for Autumn. Amens chorused around the room.

Bowls and platters were passed. Bram and Jori fought over a roll and Lorna had to trade places with Jori to separate them. Silverware clinked and voices mingled. Dan's gaze met and held Lorrie's.

Emotion filled her chest and her throat. Nothing was as important as having her family together. Nothing.

Nothing was as important as loving and being loved.

Could she call him Tom in front of others for the rest of her life? Could she come to terms with this bizarre situation and put the feelings of betrayal behind her?

"Tom," she said aloud.

Something flickered behind Dan's eyes, something uncertain and wholly alert. Tom and Cedra, the only ones who picked up on her use of the name, glanced over. Dan's attention didn't waver from her face.

"Pass the potatoes, please."

Calmly, purposefully, his expression unaltered, Dan picked up the bowl and handed it to her.

Activity went on all around them, Autumn and Jackie giggling, Gil and Orrin discussing the upcoming city elections. The whole picture was so normal, so Norman Rockwell. It was totally incongruous with the turbulent scene silently being acted out between Dan and Lorrie.

Could she remember to call him Tom? What if she slipped? Would it become second nature?

She'd called him Tom for fourteen years. What if she called him Tom when they were alone? When they were in bed?

"Thank you." She placed mashed potatoes on her and Autumn's plates and handed back the bowl, and even though her stomach had gone into a spin cycle, she took a bite.

Dan took the bowl and set it down, his heart behaving a little strangely. Why had she done that? Tom and Cedra went on with their meal, Cedra listening to Ruby's directions on how to get gravy stains out of the white tablecloth.

Lorraine helped Autumn get her fingers around her spoon. Unobtrusively, she cleaned up a blob of potatoes and gravy that hit the front of Autumn's shirt and encouraged her to try again. She ended up feeding Autumn most of her meal in between taking her own bites, and, obviously, she didn't care. It was plain to Dan that she was as happy as he was to have Autumn home.

Sure, it hurt to see her this way, but it was only a matter of weeks until she'd be back to normal. Dr. Demarco had assured them that retraining Autumn to use her muscles would be as simple as teaching a healthy toddler. The more intensive her treatment, the speedier her recovery. Dan and Lorraine had explained Autumn's condition to the boys, so none of them commented. Ruby, however, dabbed her eyes with her napkin and hurried toward the kitchen with the excuse of refilling the boys' milk glasses.

"Grampa," Thad said to Orrin, "why don't you come watch the game on TV with us next Saturday?"

"What game is that?" Lorrie's father asked.

Thad, Dan, and the twins exchanged horrified looks. Gil chuckled.

"The *Nebraska* game, of course!" Thad exclaimed. "The Huskers are heading for another national championship."

"Tom makes his special chili," Lorraine added in a coaxing voice.

Dan met her eyes.

She'd called him Tom quite naturally. He wondered if she'd even realized what she'd done. He dared to feel a little hope, but the inconsistencies of their relationship flared up at him. At one moment, like this one, it seemed their life was on course, but the next second, when they were faced head on with coming to any answers, things took a nosedive.

"Sure, I'll come for the game," Orrin decided. "What time is it?"

"You have to come in time for the *pre*-game show, Grampa," Jori informed his grandfather slowly, as if he were from another planet. The family laughed.

Later that night, after company was gone and the kids were in bed, Dan stepped to the family room doorway to check on his father. He was surprised to find Thad sitting with him.

"Can you believe Grandpa Loring didn't know about the game this week?" Thad asked.

"Not everybody's as crazy about football as you are, Thad."

"Yeah, but doesn't he watch the news? Or read the paper?" Thad scoffed.

"Sure, he watches the stock exchange."

"*Bor*-ing."

"People's interests are different," Gil said.

"I guess so."

An easy silence passed, and Dan prepared to move away.

"Don't be intolerant of other people's differences, Thad," Gil said. "Don't be like me."

Where had that come from? Dan stopped where he was and couldn't help listening.

"What do you mean?" Thad asked.

"For a long, long time I thought your dad and your uncle Dan should want the same things I wanted, should want what I wanted *for* them." He took his time, as if he was forming the words carefully. "I didn't let them decide for themselves."

Thad didn't say anything. Dan let the words soak in, guilty about eavesdropping, but not willing to miss what came next. His father had never spoken to him of these things.

"I even started trying to decide things for you. But your dad held me back."

"Like wanting me to work the orchards?" Thad asked quietly.

"Yeah."

"But now you don't want that?"

Gil's head turned toward his grandson as though he was looking into his eyes. "I still have hopes and dreams. But they're mine, not yours. I want you to do what makes you happy, Thad, not what makes me happy."

"My dad's happy," Thad said after a minute.

Gil nodded. "I believe he is. And he doesn't resent me for pushing him. He's done more with the farm than I ever could have, than I ever hoped for."

Those words evoked new emotion in Dan's chest. Pride. Gratitude. Things he'd never felt where his father was concerned.

"And he's a fine husband and father," Gil went on.

Thad nodded his head in agreement.

"You know I could never tell him and Dan apart when they were small?"

"You couldn't?" Thad's voice sounded incredulous.

"No. But I can now. Even if I couldn't see, I could tell them apart. Like he can tell Bram and Jori apart."

"You can tell Bram and Jori apart," Thad said.

"I worked at it," Gil admitted.

"So did Dad."

Gil agreed.

"He's a great dad," Thad said.

"He's a great son," Gil added.

Dan's heart swelled at his father's words. His chest filled with a sense of accomplishment he'd never known. He'd never until that moment realized how much his father's approval meant to him. He stepped into the room.

Gil and Thad looked up.

"I wish you had told me that a long time ago," Dan said to his father.

Gil looked almost embarrassed. Somehow it was easier for him to talk to Thad than to his sons. But Dan was okay with that. "It's hard to change," Gil said simply.

Dan nodded.

"I'm happy here with you and Lorrie," Gil said with a shrug.

It had always been obvious that the old man was fond of Lorraine. She was like his own daughter.

"I have more time to spend with your kids than I ever did with my own," he went on.

And Dan realized that was true. Gil had put his heart and soul into the orchards, building a legacy that was now Dan's and would remain for *his* grandchildren.

Did it matter what name his father called him? It was *Dan's* accomplishments he was proud of, *Dan's* children he took an interest in, *Dan* he thought was a good son and husband and father. *Dan.*

And at that moment Dan realized he could live with that.

A light rain pattered against the roof. "You'd better go up to bed, son."

Thad rubbed his grandfather's arm through his shirtsleeve and picked up the Game Boy on the end table. "'Night, Grampa."

After he'd gone, Dan unfolded the sofa bed and brought pillows from the cupboard. "I could turn my office into a room for you," he offered once again. "That way you'd have a little more privacy."

"I'm gonna take you up on that this time," Gil replied, surprising him. "I liked my room upstairs, but it was getting harder and harder to do all those steps."

"Good," Dan replied. "We'll do it this week. I'll call the phone company about moving my phone and fax up there. Dad."

"Yeah?"

"I don't resent anything about my childhood anymore." And it was true. His father had made mistakes, but who didn't?

"I wish your ma knew how you turned out," Gil said.

"I'm sure she does."

His father nodded. "'Night, son."

"'Night, Dad." He took the stairs two at a time, feeling more unburdened than he had in years. After all this time his life was coming together. There was only one more thing he needed to work out. And finally...*finally,* he had an idea of how to do it.

"We haven't done this for a long time," Lorrie commented.

"Feels good, eh?" Dan asked.

The hostess at the Lied Center dining room led the two of them to a table by the windows and told them what the silver-domed buffet dishes held that noon.

"It is different getting away without the kids, and on a weekday, too," Lorrie said after the girl had gone. She'd been surprised when Dan had asked her.

"Cedra and Gil were happy to stay with Autumn. Tom went into Omaha for bike parts."

"He's become obsessed with that bike, hasn't he?"

Dan shrugged.

They ordered the buffet and helped themselves to the delicious entrees, vegetables and dessert. Afterward, they sipped coffee.

A few other diners ate in the spacious sunlit room, decorated with antique cabinets and crockery, but none were seated nearby.

"I didn't sleep very well," Dan admitted.

"You should have been exhausted."

"I was. But I couldn't stop thinking about overhearing Thad and my father last night." He'd related the conversation to Lorrie when he'd come to bed.

"We're never too old to change, I guess," she said.

His eyes appeared more blue in the sunlight streaming through the window. His gaze moved from her face to her fingers on her cup. "I realized that offhand recognition is enough for me," he went on. "It doesn't matter what he thinks my name is. You were right. I was caught up in having him acknowledge me as Dan, but I *am* Dan. Just because he calls me Tom doesn't change who I really am."

Lorrie stared at him for a full minute.

Dan raised his eyes and shifted under her scrutiny.

"In other words, you're okay with being known as Tom?"

He nodded.

"What about Tom?"

"I talked to him this morning before he left. He's actually sympathetic to what we're going through here, and he's content with being Buzz. He's called himself Buzz for years. In fact, he's thinking of having his name legally changed."

Lorrie's eyes widened with disbelief. She blinked and turned to stare out the windows at the breathtaking fall scenery for several minutes. When she turned back, Dan's heart was in his eyes. The uncertainty and vulnerability struck a responsive chord in her heart. "Have you thought about that?" she asked.

"What?"

"Having your name legally changed?"

He nodded.

She took a deep breath and gathered her thoughts. "How would that make things . . . right?"

"The only ones it makes a difference for are the kids, right?" he asked. "They are the only reason I don't just tell everyone the truth. And for you, Lorraine. I don't want you humiliated."

"I'm sorry about that," she hurried to say. "I'm sorry I panicked and threatened you the way I did. I've felt terrible about it ever since. I wouldn't . . . I couldn't..." Tears threatened and she fought them, blinking.

He covered her hand with his. "Wait for me. I'll be right back."

She nodded, gathered her composure, and watched him walk to the far side of the room, pay the cashier and slip out the door. Several minutes later, he returned. "Come on."

She picked up her purse and followed.

Dan took her hand and led her past the hotel registration desk. One of the young women stared, then turned and whispered something to the woman beside her.

"What are they staring at?" Lorrie asked.

"Tom told me how nice the rooms are here. They probably think I bring a different woman every week."

Lorrie turned from the gaping women to Dan, not finding the mistaken identity amusing. "You mean they think—you—that we're...?"

Dan pulled her down a long hallway and slid a key in a lock. "Does it matter what they think when we know the truth?"

She let him usher her into the room. That was the whole crux of the matter, wasn't it? That was how they were going to be able to deal with this. By not caring what others thought, as long as the two of them knew the truth. "No. I guess it doesn't," she conceded aloud.

Finally, she took stock of her surroundings and glanced around the elegantly furnished suite. "What are we doing here?"

"I think you wanted to tell me something. I have something to say, too, and I thought it might be easier to do it where we'd be alone. I mean, really alone. No one knows we're here...well, except for those two at the desk, and I don't think they really care." The side of his mouth quirked up.

He opened a window overlooking the fall-dressed countryside. A fresh breeze filled the room and he came back to sit on the edge of the bed.

Lorrie tossed her purse on a low table, slipped off her shoes, and propped herself against the headboard. "Not as comfortable as our bed."

His gaze moved from her eyes to her hair, then slid down her body to the bare legs she'd raised to the bed. He pulled her feet into his lap and massaged them. "Tell me now, Lorraine."

"What?"

"What you started to say out there. Were you going to say... that you wouldn't have left me?"

How she'd cursed herself for that rash statement! "Surely you knew," she said softly, "that I didn't mean it."

"I would have deserved it," he replied. "You were right. I was trying to appease myself at your expense, at the children's expense. You were just trying to protect them."

"All of that," she said, pulling her feet behind her and leaning toward him, "was so unimportant... so *trivial* compared to what's of real value here."

"And what's that?"

Her feelings were so intense, she was afraid to look him in the eye. She studied the coverlet. "Our family," she whispered. "Our children."

He waited silently.

"When I thought Autumn was going to... going to—"

"Don't—"

"Die," she choked out. "I knew then that none of this really mattered. Not when it was in perspective. You saved her life," she whispered, still experiencing the same awe.

"I only did what I had to," he said.

"You did what I couldn't."

"That doesn't matter."

"It does to me."

"If I hadn't been there, you would have been able to do what you had to."

She shook her head. "I don't know."

"That's not why you changed your mind?" he questioned roughly. "Because I knew how to help Autumn."

She looked up then. "Of course not! But that's what showed me. You're her father. You're my husband." A well of thick emotion rose to her throat. "You're a father to the twins. You've made it a personal goal to be especially sensitive to their needs."

"Because I knew how it felt."

"Regardless of why, you've done it. And—Thad," she managed to say around a lump of tears.

Dan didn't move. Didn't try to hold her gaze when she dropped it to his chest.

"All those years you thought he was Tom's child. You thought I'd conceived him with your brother. But you loved him anyway." Her voice still held a note of awe. "You were a father to him anyway." The last was a whisper.

Lorrie looked up and saw his tears. "How that must have hurt you." Her own tear ran down her nose to her lip and she caught it with her tongue. "And when I told you the truth, you made a decision to forgive me." A sob caught in her throat.

Dan reached for her face, and she grasped his wrist and nuzzled her cheek against his palm. "I love you," he said hoarsely.

"You love me crazy," she said to him. "You love me in a way that makes you pretend to be someone you're not just to have me. And the way you love lets you forgive and keep loving."

"Well, then I guess you must love me crazy, too." He rubbed his thumb across her lips. "Because after you knew I was Dan, you still slept with me and made love to me. I know you love me."

She had never denied it.

"The only question is whether or not you love me enough to forgive me."

She studied the blue eyes that waited with the tragic question in their depths. She regarded the face she knew so well—lips she'd kissed a million times, the silver hair above his ears that hadn't been there when they'd first become lovers. Love him enough to forgive him? She was ashamed of herself for making him wonder, for making him wait.

His thumb traced her lower lip.

For the first time she realized she'd been ashamed of needing him so much that forgiving him had always been the only thing she *wanted* to do.

She loved Daniel Beckett. And about that, there was no choice.

Chapter 14

"Well?"

Lorrie recognized the apprehension in the word, in his eyes. "I don't want to lose you," she said. "I don't want to lose us."

His hand slid from her cheek and caressed her fingers. He brought them to his lips and kissed her knuckles.

"I was ashamed of how much I needed you," she confessed. "Like I thought I would somehow lose my dignity by wanting you even though you'd done this awful thing."

"It was awful," he said. "I know that. And it's okay for you to say it to me. That first day, when you were so mad, it absolved me somehow. I deserved your anger. After that, when you got over being mad, I had to see your hurt. I knew how disappointed and…disillusioned you were with me. Mad was easier to deal with."

Lorrie grazed her fingertips over his lips and across his cheek, outlining the face she loved so well, bringing her touch back to his lips. "I want to put our life back together," she said. "And I forgive you."

His mouth stilled on her fingers. He raised his eyes to hers. Lorrie waited for him to say something. Releasing her hand, he shifted to one hip and drew his wallet from his pocket. Curious, Lorrie watched him open it and shake something from the key flap. Her wedding rings fell into his palm.

He held them toward her in his long fingers. "Will you marry me?"

She knew, as she'd always known but had been too proud to see, that this was the man she loved with all her heart. It didn't matter what his name was as long as he loved her. She held her hand out and steadied it while he slid the rings on her finger. "I don't have yours with me," she whispered with regret.

"You can give it to me on our wedding day." He covered her lips with his and Lorrie tasted tears—hers or his, she didn't know.

"I can't make up for all the hurt I caused you," he whispered against her cheek.

She cupped his face and kissed him hard, kissed him fervently, with all the need and want and desperation welling in her heart. "I forgive you," she said again with barely a pause.

Catching her intensity, Dan pushed her back on the bed, urging her mouth wider and engaging her tongue in an erotic match. He always made her feel this way— sexy, eager, aglow with love for him. Wanting more, she reached for his shirt, unfastened the buttons, and pushed the fabric from his shoulders.

Dan yanked the shirt from his jeans and shrugged out of it, pulling her cotton top over her head and coaxing her out of her shorts, while kissing her neck and shoulders.

He tugged the band from her braid and loosened her hair with his fingers. "I should have told you from the beginning," he said.

Lorrie caught his face between both palms and held him still. "You're going to have to make me some promises."

"Okay."

"No more regrets. No more guilt. They've eaten at you for too long, and that's behind us. You can't be any sorrier than you are. I can't be any sorrier than I am. We just go on from here."

Beneath her hands, his cheeks were warm and slightly rough, a delicious texture. "Okay."

"Promise me, Beckett."

He touched her hair. "I promise."

"Good. Enough of that sorry stuff, then." She led his lips back to hers and wrapped her arms around his solid shoulders.

Dan pressed her back on the bed, running his wonderful hands over her skin. She helped him ease off her underclothing and pulled back the bedding while he removed his jeans and briefs.

He slid his warm solid length alongside her and held her close.

"This feels absolutely decadent," she sighed. "Broad daylight and no one expecting us."

"We should do this more often."

"We couldn't do this any more often. We'd wear ourselves out." She smiled against his shoulder.

"I didn't mean *this*—" he almost said, but she cut him off with a kiss. He returned the kiss, took control of it, pulling her tongue against his and stealing her breath.

He shifted and sat back so he could cup her breasts, one in each hand, lifting, weighing, brushing his rough palms against her sensitive nipples. He made her feel desirable and on fire, as he always did. She smiled and ran her hands up his arms to his shoulders, loving the play of flesh and muscle.

Dan spanned her waist, kissed her navel, and his hair, cool and silky, brushed her stomach. She threaded her fingers through the mass and sighed at the wild pleasure his hands and lips built in her body. Lorrie closed her eyes and gave herself over to her lover.

He moved to sit at her feet and kissed her ankles, ran his tongue along her soles and kissed the insides of her knees. An exquisite shudder rippled through her legs and her nipples pebbled with desire.

Dan reached up to roll one and then the other between his thumb and forefinger. Lorrie opened her eyes and found his glittering with excitement, his lips wet and parted.

He held her gaze; his breath touched her hip, her breast. He moved up, taking one peak in his mouth and bestowing lavish pleasure. He touched her purposefully, intimately, revering and wooing, his caress ardent yet tender. Lorrie caught her breath and surrendered to the erotic delight. She clutched the sheets and groaned, spinning...out of control.

Dan...was always...the one in control. If only...she could...make him...lose his composure, see him...unable to hold back. Maybe...maybe...she did hold the power....

A shivery tremor of delight coursed through Lorraine's body. Dan loved the way she moved and the sounds she made, the smell of her skin and the taste of her eagerness. There was nothing more beautiful than his Lorraine.

She turned slightly. "I want you in me now, Dan," she rasped. "I don't want to wait."

Her words reached him at the same time her hands grasped at his shoulders.

"Now, Dan...now..."

Dan sank deep inside her, drawn by her movements and her voice and her straining impatience.

He'd always prided himself in taking her to the edge and keeping her there, prolonging her enjoyment. He'd never been unable to hold back, never been helpless to the demand of his body and her soft cries.

She kissed him, enveloped him, sapping his strength and control.

"Dan," she panted against his mouth, "*now*, Dan." She gasped and arched.

He was powerless to hold back...powerless.... He throbbed into her in a heedless burst of ecstasy.

With his face buried in her neck, he allowed the wash of feelings to suffuse him. Humble. Complete. Embarrassed.

She surprised him by shifting in his embrace and rolling him to his back. She leaned above him, her silky hair flowing across his chest. The skin of her face and neck and even her breasts was exquisitely flushed. Her warm honey eyes held an amazing glow. She kissed his chest, one nipple, slid up and plucked kisses along his neck and his jaw. "I love you, Daniel Beckett."

He couldn't say anything. Fourteen years of restraint welled up and prevented anything he might have thought to reply. He touched her hair and finally, when the wave of emotion ebbed, he spoke. "I love you, Lorraine."

She kissed his lips. "When shall we do it?"

"You'll have to give me a few minutes, babe—"

"Get *married*," she said with a mock blow to his ribs.

"Oh." He cradled one hand behind his head and rubbed her shoulder with the other. "We could tell everyone we're renewing our vows," he suggested.

She trailed a finger through the hair on his chest. "We'd have to wait until our anniversary for that."

"Hm-mm. We could elope."

She raised her brows. "That seems to suggest we have something to be ashamed of."

He studied her, wondering where her thoughts were leading. "I could have my name legally changed," he said. "But if we apply for a license, our names will be in the paper."

"And you don't want to cause me any embarrassment," she replied.

No, he didn't. And she'd already made her feelings perfectly clear about letting anyone else know. He shrugged.

"I was wrapped up in my own personal drama when I threatened you." Her palm flattened against his chest. "I couldn't cope with it all right then. If others had known before I'd come to terms with it myself, I couldn't have handled it."

Dan drew his hand from behind his head and held her by both upper arms. "What are you saying?"

"I'm saying—" she tucked her hair behind one ear "—we need to tell the truth."

Dan's heart felt like his stomach did when he rode an elevator. Lorraine's eyes didn't waver from his. "Do you know what you're saying?"

"Yes."

"What about all the people who will be hurt?"

"Who?" she asked. "Who will be hurt?"

"Well, the kids—"

"The kids know that you're their father. They call you Dad anyway. Children are more accepting than adults."

"You don't think they'd feel as betrayed as you did?"

"No, I don't. They didn't even exist when you made that decision. Thad might require a little more explanation, but I'm sure he'll understand when he hears the whole story."

"The *whole* story?"

"He doesn't have to know that you thought he was Tom's. That, or what name you go by, has no effect on his life now."

"My father . . . your parents . . ."

"Gil is the one person who should know. And everyone else will just have to accept it. Are you worrying now about what they'll think of you?"

Maybe he was.

"I think I was the one with the most at stake, and I still love you," she said. "Tom and Cedra accepted it and love you. Why would anyone else be different? And if they are, do they matter? You have a sound standing in this community, and that will go a long way."

He loosened his hold on her arms and brushed his palms over her shoulders. "And you?" he asked. "Will you be okay with everyone knowing?"

She turned her cheek against his fingers. "I don't think others will pick apart all the legalities like we were forced to do. I'm proud to be your wife, Dan, and in my heart I am your wife. A wedding will simply make it legal."

"Would a wedding make you happy?"

"You make me happy."

He cupped her head and raised his to kiss her. The kiss was a solemn affirmation, sealing their plans and their commitment. There would be an initial discomfort involved with revealing the truth, but they would weather it together, and in the long run there would be no more hiding.

Dan hadn't anticipated the relief he experienced now. His grin ended their kiss.

She placed one finger against his lower lip. "So it really excites you for me to call you Dan, eh?" She slid her body against his.

"It was the only thing missing between us all this time," he said softly.

"Dan..." Her eyes widened. "Dan!"

Epilogue

"Are you sure these guys are really ever gonna come out of here?" Cedra rubbed her enormous belly and collapsed into a lawn chair a safe distance from where Dan stood, grilling hamburgers. Aromatic smoke billowed around his head and drifted on the Indian summer breeze.

"I'm positive," Lorrie reassured her, handed her a glass of lemonade and secured all the plates and cups on the picnic table. The boys had set up the badminton set and were arguing over who went first. "No one has ever been perpetually pregnant."

Cedra took a sip and watched Autumn, playing with her dolls on a blanket nearby. "These babies are already fighting and jostling each other."

"*This,* my dear sister-in-law, before they're born, is the easy part. Relax and enjoy it."

"Enjoy it? I haven't seen anything below my navel for four months. I'm retaining enough water in this heat to

fill your swimming pool, *and—*" she lowered her voice
and leaned forward "my sex life is *definitely* in a
slump."

"Ah," Lorrie said, sympathetically. "This, too, shall
pass."

"And I'll have my own body back?"

"Assuredly."

"I guess I have to believe you." Cedra leaned back.
"You've been through it and you and Dan still have the
hots for each other."

Lorrie laughed and settled into a chair beside her. Her
gaze wavered to Autumn, now completely recovered,
and noted how she slid the clothes on her dolls and
snapped the fasteners without a problem. Never a day
went by that Lorrie didn't say a prayer of thanks for
Autumn's life.

And a prayer of thanks for Dan.

Her husband used his hat to fan the fire, raised his
head and caught her watching him. An involuntary
smile made him raise his brows and grin. "What are you
two talking about?"

"How hot it is for this time of year," she called back.

Beside her, Cedra chuckled.

Lorrie hadn't thought she and Dan could be any
closer, but saying their vows before their family and
friends had held more meaning than either of them expected. This time around, they knew what marriage was
all about: they understood sickness and health, richer
and poorer, and cleaving one to the other.

After an initial explanation, the children had been as
accepting as Lorrie had hoped. Thad had voiced a few
questions, but from his own experience with Gil, he
understood.

Lorrie's family had been shocked at the news, but because of their deep love for their daughter and for Dan, they'd done their best to be supportive. The community was still a bit puzzled, yet they were beginning to accept Dan's new name. Even if their midwestern neighbors hadn't been as understanding as they seemed, Lorrie knew she and Dan would still be better off for having told the truth.

They had no secrets from each other or from anyone else. They didn't have to live with the risk of accidentally using the wrong name or being discovered. Peace of mind was well worth any minor embarrassment. And through it all, their love had survived and grown.

They weren't unrealistic enough to think that there wouldn't be rocky times ahead with elderly parents and, before they knew it, a house full of teenagers. But they were confident they could handle the future together.

Having Tom near had given Dan an additional sense of peace. Lorrie gave her attention back to Cedra. "It was great of you guys to come help with the Festival again this year."

"I only wish I could have helped pick," Cedra said. "Everybody's treating me like I'm something special, making me stay in the house or in the air-conditioned gift shop."

"You are special, Cedra."

Her sister-in-law smiled, a smile of contentment and well-being. "I never felt that way until Buzz. And then you guys. A couple of years ago, I couldn't have imagined my life the way it is now, I mean with a family and a husband and a baby. It's pretty mind-blowing."

Lorrie knew how Dan made her feel. If Tom came anywhere near being the husband his brother was, it was no wonder Cedra glowed. "Dan—and Gil—are both so glad that you and Buzz decided to stay nearby."

Tom had started his own cycle shop in Omaha and they made regular visits to Beckett Orchards. The entire family had rejoiced over their announcement of Cedra's pregnancy, and then again when her ultrasound showed twin boys.

"Where *are* Buzz and Gil?" Lorrie asked.

"Buzz has a little surprise for Dan," Cedra said mysteriously. She'd no sooner answered and Tom's beat-up truck rolled up the drive with Gil driving. The old man got out and walked toward them.

Gil's reaction had been the one Dan had worried about the most. He'd asked her to sit with them while he told his father, and she'd been grateful. Gil's expression had been thunderstruck, and because she knew Dan so well, she knew he was experiencing a pang of regret.

Gil had asked surprisingly few questions, and once those were answered to his satisfaction he'd said, "This explains so much. I thought I was losing my mind."

"What do you mean, Dad?"

"Those damned birthday cakes, for one thing." He turned to Lorrie and she smiled.

Then he studied Dan's face. "You told me you loved it here and that you weren't sorry I made you stay and work the farm. You really meant that."

"I did."

"The Tom I knew wouldn't have meant it. Wouldn't have done it. Sometimes I thought . . ."

"Thought what, Dad?"

"I thought I'd broken Tom's spirit."

Dan laid his hand on his father's arm. "Tom's too strong for that."

"But I did drive him away."

Dan didn't deny it.

"And I wasn't fair."

Still Dan said nothing.

"That was wrong, I know."

"Dad, nobody's to blame for any of this. Lorraine and I made a promise to each other. No more regrets, no more sorrys."

Gil turned a watery gaze on Lorrie.

"You have to promise, too," Dan went on. "We don't look back with regret for what we did or didn't do. It got us where we are right now, and where we are is pretty darned good."

"Thank you for telling me, son," Gil had said, his voice choked with emotion. "Thanks, Danny."

Dan hadn't been able to speak.

As old and as set in his ways as Gil was, he'd done a fair job of making amends to both of his sons over the past months.

Now Lorrie watched Gil approaching and asked Cedra, "What's he doing?"

"He just drove back from the tractor barn. That's where Buzz hid his truck earlier."

"Well, where is Tom?"

Just then, a low purring engine rumbled across the countryside, and along with everyone else, Lorrie looked toward the sound. Tom rode an enormous Harley up the driveway. Sunlight caught the chrome and mirrors and reflected off the glossy black paint. He rolled to a stop and killed the engine. The sound echoed in the distance.

Thad, Bram and Jori ran to their uncle with appreciative shouts. Dan turned from the smoking grill and approached, thumbing his black hat brim back and grinning. "Hey, you finally did it."

Tom, wearing a Husker ball cap backward, matched his grin. "Yup."

Dan walked around the Harley with admiration. "Nice job, Buzz."

"Thanks, Dan." Tom reached to the ignition and pulled the key out. He took a few steps and dangled it in front of his brother. "It's yours."

The surprise on Dan's face was genuine. He frowned first, a look of confusion, and then a blank realization claimed his features. "What?"

"It's for you."

A second passed. None of the children spoke. They looked from their uncle to their father. Gil wore a knowing grin. Finally, Dan's hand came out and he took the keys. "What will I do with a bike?"

"Do whatever you want with it," Tom replied. "It's yours."

Lorrie didn't know if she understood the significance of the brothers' exchange. Years ago the bike had been Dan's. He'd given it to his brother, a young man with wanderlust in his veins, and watched him leave. Now, years later, his brother was back and he intended to stay. The bike had served its purpose, eventually bringing Tom back to the family.

"This is so cool!" Thad exclaimed. "Will you take me for a ride, Dad?"

Dan and Tom exchanged looks. Tom loped over to his pickup and returned with two shiny new helmets.

Dan looked to Lorrie. "Lorraine—?"

"I'll watch the burgers."

He tossed Bram his hat and the Harley roared down the drive.

Tom bent low and kissed Cedra. "I think he liked it."

Gil picked up the metal spatula and winked at Lorrie. "I think he liked it."

Lorrie gazed at the bike, appearing and disappearing between patches of glorious red sumac along the highway, and smiled to herself. "I think he liked it."

The burgers were done and the meal half-eaten when they returned. Dan, smelling of country air and hickory smoke, wrapped his arms around Lorrie from behind. "You're next, babe."

She leaned back into his strong embrace. "I don't know..."

He kissed her ear. "You don't have to."

If he'd coaxed her, it would have been easier to turn him down. But in letting her make up her own mind, he'd made it more of a challenge. She turned in his embrace. "All right. Call me crazy."

He grinned. "I'll call you sexy like I always have."

His smile still did wild things to her heart. He was the same man she'd always loved, but his recently regained identity had given him a new and appealing confidence. She followed him and took the helmet he handed her.

"I know a deserted little spot down by the brook in the east orchard..." he said with a suggestive lift of one brow. "And you can call me ready, willing and able."

She laughed and straddled the bike, wrapping her arms around his waist and hugging him. "All I ever want to call you is... mine."

* * * * *

FAST CASH 4031 DRAW RULES
NO PURCHASE OR OBLIGATION NECESSARY

Fifty prizes of $50 each will be awarded in random drawings to be conducted no later than 3/28/97 from amongst all eligible responses to this prize offer received as of 2/14/97. To enter, follow directions, affix 1st-class postage and mail OR write Fast Cash 4031 on a 3" x 5" card along with your name and address and mail that card to: Harlequin's Fast Cash 4031 Draw, P.O. Box 1395, Buffalo, NY 14240-1395 OR P.O. Box 618, Fort Erie, Ontario L2A 5X3. (Limit: one entry per outer envelope; all entries must be sent via 1st-class mail.) Limit: one prize per household. Odds of winning are determined by the number of eligible responses received. Offer is open only to residents of the U.S. (except Puerto Rico) and Canada and is void wherever prohibited by law. All applicable laws and regulations apply. Any litigation within the province of Quebec respecting the conduct and awarding of a prize in this sweepstakes maybe submitted to the Régie des alcools, des courses et des jeux. In order for a Canadian resident to win a prize, that person will be required to correctly answer a time-limited arithmetical skill-testing question to be administered by mail. Names of winners available after 4/28/97 by sending a self-addressed, stamped envelope to: Fast Cash 4031 Draw Winners, P.O. Box 4200, Blair, NE 68009-4200.

OFFICIAL RULES
MILLION DOLLAR SWEEPSTAKES
NO PURCHASE NECESSARY TO ENTER

1. To enter, follow the directions published. Method of entry may vary. For eligibility, entries must be received no later than March 31, 1998. No liability is assumed for printing errors, lost, late, non-delivered or misdirected entries.

   To determine winners, the sweepstakes numbers assigned to submitted entries will be compared against a list of randomly pre-selected prize winning numbers. In the event all prizes are not claimed via the return of prize winning numbers, random drawings will be held from among all other entries received to award unclaimed prizes.

2. Prize winners will be determined no later than June 30, 1998. Selection of winning numbers and random drawings are under the supervision of D. L. Blair, Inc., an independent judging organization whose decisions are final. Limit: one prize to a family or organization. No substitution will be made for any prize, except as offered. Taxes and duties on all prizes are the sole responsibility of winners. Winners will be notified by mail. Odds of winning are determined by the number of eligible entries distributed and received.

3. Sweepstakes open to residents of the U.S. (except Puerto Rico), Canada and Europe who are 18 years of age or older, except employees and immediate family members of Torstar Corp., D. L. Blair, Inc., their affiliates, subsidiaries, and all other agencies, entities, and persons connected with the use, marketing or conduct of this sweepstakes. All applicable laws and regulations apply. Sweepstakes offer void wherever prohibited by law. Any litigation within the province of Quebec respecting the conduct and awarding of a prize in this sweepstakes must be submitted to the Régie des alcools, des courses et des jeux. In order to win a prize, residents of Canada will be required to correctly answer a time-limited arithmetical skill-testing question to be administered by mail.

4. Winners of major prizes (Grand through Fourth) will be obligated to sign and return an Affidavit of Eligibility and Release of Liability within 30 days of notification. In the event of non-compliance within this time period or if a prize is returned as undeliverable, D. L. Blair, Inc. may at its sole discretion award that prize to an alternate winner. By acceptance of their prize, winners consent to use of their names, photographs or other likeness for purposes of advertising, trade and promotion on behalf of Torstar Corp., its affiliates and subsidiaries, without further compensation unless prohibited by law. Torstar Corp. and D. L. Blair, Inc., their affiliates and subsidiaries are not responsible for errors in printing of sweepstakes and prizewinning numbers. In the event a duplication of a prizewinning number occurs, a random drawing will be held from among all entries received with that prizewinning number to award that prize.

SWP-S12ZD1

5. This sweepstakes is presented by Torstar Corp., its subsidiaries and affiliates in conjunction with book, merchandise and/or product offerings. The number of prizes to be awarded and their value are as follows: Grand Prize — $1,000,000 (payable at $33,333.33 a year for 30 years); First Prize — $50,000; Second Prize — $10,000; Third Prize — $5,000; 3 Fourth Prizes — $1,000 each; 10 Fifth Prizes — $250 each; 1,000 Sixth Prizes — $10 each. Values of all prizes are in U.S. currency. Prizes in each level will be presented in different creative executions, including various currencies, vehicles, merchandise and travel. Any presentation of a prize level in a currency other than U.S. currency represents an approximate equivalent to the U.S. currency prize for that level, at that time. Prize winners will have the opportunity of selecting any prize offered for that level; however, the actual non U.S. currency equivalent prize, if offered and selected, shall be awarded at the exchange rate existing at 3:00 P.M. New York time on March 31, 1998. A travel prize option, if offered and selected by winner, must be completed within 12 months of selection and is subject to: traveling companion(s) completing and returning a Release of Liability prior to travel; and hotel and flight accommodations availability. For a current list of all prize options offered within prize levels, send a self-addressed, stamped envelope (WA residents need not affix postage) to: MILLION DOLLAR SWEEPSTAKES Prize Options, P.O. Box 4456, Blair, NE 68009-4456, USA.

6. For a list of prize winners (available after July 31, 1998) send a separate, stamped, self-addressed envelope to: MILLION DOLLAR SWEEPSTAKES Winners, P.O. Box 4459, Blair, NE 68009-4459, USA.

EXTRA BONUS PRIZE DRAWING
NO PURCHASE OR OBLIGATION NECESSARY TO ENTER

7. The Extra Bonus Prize will be awarded in a random drawing to be conducted no later than 5/30/98 from among all entries received. To qualify, entries must be received by 3/31/98 and comply with published directions. Prize ($50,000) is valued in U.S. currency. Prize will be presented in different creative expressions, including various currencies, vehicles, merchandise and travel. Any presentation in a currency other than U.S. currency represents an approximate equivalent to the U.S. currency value at that time. Prize winner will have the opportunity of selecting any prize offered in any presentation of the Extra Bonus Prize Drawing; however, the actual non U.S. currency equivalent prize, if offered and selected by winner, shall be awarded at the exchange rate existing at 3:00 P.M. New York time on March 31, 1998. For a current list of prize options offered, send a self-addressed, stamped envelope (WA residents need not affix postage) to: Extra Bonus Prize Options, P.O. Box 4462, Blair, NE 68009-4462, USA. All eligibility requirements and restrictions of the MILLION DOLLAR SWEEPSTAKES apply. Odds of winning are dependent upon number of eligible entries received. No substitution for prize except as offered. For the name of winner (available after 7/31/98), send a self-addressed, stamped envelope to: Extra Bonus Prize Winner, P.O. Box 4463, Blair, NE 68009-4463, USA.

SWP-S12ZD2

In February, Silhouette Books is proud
to present the sweeping, sensual new novel
by bestselling author

CAIT LONDON

about her unforgettable family—*The Tallchiefs*.

Everyone in Amen Flats, Wyoming, was talking about
Elspeth Tallchief. How she wasn't a thirty-three-year-old
virgin, after all. How she'd been keeping herself warm at
night all these years with a couple of secrets. And now one
of those secrets had walked right into town, sending
everyone into a frenzy. But Elspeth knew he'd come for
the *other* secret....

"Cait London is an irresistible storyteller..."
—*Romantic Times*

Don't miss TALLCHIEF FOR KEEPS by Cait London, available
at your favorite retail outlet in February from

Silhouette®

CLST

As seen on TV!
Free Gift Offer

With a Free Gift proof-of-purchase from any Silhouette® book,
you can receive a beautiful cubic zirconia pendant.

This gorgeous marquise-shaped stone is a genuine cubic
zirconia—accented by an 18" gold tone necklace.

(Approximate retail value $19.95)

Send for yours today...
compliments of ▼ *Silhouette*®

To receive your free gift, a cubic zirconia pendant, send us one original proof-of-
purchase, photocopies not accepted, from the back of any Silhouette Romance™,
Silhouette Desire®, Silhouette Special Edition®, Silhouette Intimate Moments®
or Silhouette Yours Truly™ title available in August, September, October, November and
December at your favorite retail outlet, together with the Free Gift Certificate, plus a
check or money order for $1.65 U.S./$2.15 CAN. (do not send cash) to cover postage and
handling, payable to Silhouette Free Gift Offer. We will send you the specified gift. Allow
6 to 8 weeks for delivery. Offer good until December 31, 1996 or while quantities last.
Offer valid in the U.S. and Canada only.

Free Gift Certificate

Name: _____

Address: _____

City: _____ State/Province: _____ Zip/Postal Code: _____

Mail this certificate, one proof-of-purchase and a check or money order for postage
and handling to: SILHOUETTE FREE GIFT OFFER 1996. In the U.S.: 3010 Walden
Avenue, P.O. Box 9077, Buffalo NY 14269-9077. In Canada: P.O. Box 613, Fort Erie,
Ontario L2Z 5X3.

FREE GIFT OFFER   084-KMD
ONE PROOF-OF-PURCHASE
To collect your fabulous FREE GIFT, a cubic zirconia pendant, you must include this
original proof-of-purchase for each gift with the properly completed Free Gift Certificate.

084-KMD-R

The collection of the year!
NEW YORK TIMES BESTSELLING AUTHORS

Linda Lael Miller
Wild About Harry

Janet Dailey
Sweet Promise

Elizabeth Lowell
Reckless Love

Penny Jordan
Love's Choices

and featuring
Nora Roberts
The Calhoun Women

This special trade-size edition features four of the wildly
popular titles in the Calhoun miniseries together in
one volume—a true collector's item!

Pick up these great authors and a chance to win
a weekend for two in New York City at the
Marriott Marquis Hotel on Broadway! We'll pay
for your flight, your hotel—even a Broadway show!

Available in December at your favorite retail outlet.

NEW YORK

MARQUIS

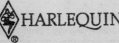

NYT1296-R